BATTLE SCARS

BATTLE SCARS

BATTLE SCARS

Jamie L. Chester

iUniverse, Inc.
New York   Bloomington

Battle Scars

iUniverse books may be ordered through booksellers or by contacting:

iUniverse
1663 Liberty Drive
Bloomington, IN 47403
www.iuniverse.com
1-800-Authors (1-800-288-4677)

Because of the dynamic nature of the Internet, any Web addresses or links contained
in this book may have changed since publication and may no longer be valid.
The views expressed in this work are solely those of the author and do not
necessarily reflect the views of the publisher, and the publisher hereby disclaims
any responsibility for them.

ISBN: 978-1-4502-0369-2 (sc)
ISBN: 978-1-4502-0368-5 (ebk)

Library of Congress Control Number: 2009914221

Printed in the United States of America

iUniverse rev. date: 01/04/2010

Rangers Lead The Way!

In the early morning rain.
In the early morning rain.
Airborne Ranger Black Beret.
You know he's here to save the day.
Deep inside he has no fear.
Because his Ranger God is near.

> Ranger Cadence.

When Jim Hunter made it through RIP, the Ranger Indoctrination Program, he thought he was ready for anything. He had proven his skills, stamina, and metal to be selected for one of the most elite units in the world, but would it be enough to survive on the battlefield?

Hunter finds himself fighting a war on two fronts, battling a ruthless determined enemy in the jungles and cities of Central America, as well as demons within himself. Follow him from the harrowing combat parachute jump on Rio Hato Airfield, through raids, a hostage extraction, and enemy interdiction operations.

To Roy, until we meet again on the other side of the objective.
Rangers Lead the Way!

To Melissa, Holden, Garrett and Gracie, thanks for making everyday
a wonderful adventure. You are my inspiration.

To Tammy, thanks for helping me, not just on the book, but in life.
I couldn't ask for a better sister.

The Enlightenment, Trials Of Life

Many times in life our souls are shaped through trials by fire. The resolve woven in the fabric of our being, the goodness within, and the integrity of our character is molded by destiny. Who among us knows when destiny will call, or what it will bestow upon our life? Sometimes one's soul is left empty, waiting for something to fill it or for one golden glorious arrow to end it.

BOOK 1

BOOK I

CHAPTER 1

The Day of Reckoning

December 20th 1989, Rio Hato Panama, Operation Just Cause - Invasion of Panama.

A song kept playing, over and over. It was like a broken record. The same lines. You would think the rest of the song would come, but it wouldn't. It was something from the 70's. "Those good old boys were drinking whisky and rye, singing this will be the day that I die, this will be the day that I die." He couldn't remember the name of the song. He didn't think he had even heard it in years, but the lines played on.

Am I ready to die? Hunter asked himself the question again as the deafening sound of the C130 aircraft's props droned on. For months it seemed, maybe even years, he had waited for this chance. To die with honor, to bring honor to his family and his memory. He had wished for this chance; now it seemed God had given it to him. The never-ending pain that seemed to tangle his lonely soul would finally end. He was not worried about the physical pain that might be involved in the process. Hunter had learned to make a friend of the pain. As twisted as it seemed, he started to really enjoy it, especially when others would fail because of it. It made him stronger. "But have I finished everything that I should have in this life?" he asked himself.

"When was the last time I told my family that I loved them?" He thought he did the last time he was home, about six months ago. Did they know he loved them? They should. His family had never really been big on saying the words, or showing the physical affection. But he was sure they knew, *didn't they?*

He hadn't made out a will. He always meant to, but the opportunity was never quite at hand. He didn't have much anyway. There were things he should have divvied out to his friends at home, even though he had felt distanced from them for years. His friends now, almost like brothers, were here with him on one of the eleven aircraft headed south to Rio Hato. It seemed comforting, although many of them would probably die with him tonight.

I want to go to heaven, and I do believe it exists, he thought. Maybe not exactly like some of the hypocrite Jesus freaks preach about, but he knew there was a place. There must be. But will I be allowed to go there when I have killed these bad guys? They are bad people. It's my job. I will meet the enemies of my country and defeat them with a vengeance they have never known; I am my country's sword. Questions raced through his mind. "But will I get into heaven?"

Although his given name was Jim Hunter, everyone usually just called him Hunter. He wondered if any of his friends now even knew what his first name was. Ever since he had enlisted in the military it seemed that was his only tag, except for his rank of course. Even back in his high school days, few people ever just called him Jim. When the Rambo movies first came out, someone had inadvertently referred to him as Jambo, and it just stuck. Who would have thought three years ago that he would be smashed into the cargo hold of a military transport as part of one of the most elite special operations units in the World? Covered in camouflage, face painted green, armed to the teeth, getting ready to jump out of an airplane into combat.

It was in high school that Hunter had begun to stand out from the crowd, showing an exceptional willingness to excel. Excel in sports, in school, and in life. He had gone to a small rural school in what many of his buddies now called "BFE." (Bum Fucked Egypt - in the middle of nowhere) In a small school it had been easy to stand out, sometimes too easy. He had learned the hard way about the consequences of complacency.

Coming off a great football season his sophomore year, Hunter had felt invincible. He had earned his varsity letter, one of only two people to do so at his age level, and was raring to wrestle. That indestructibility that he had felt in football had carried directly onto the wrestling mat. He was on top of the world, and it seemed that he was destined to stay that way.

Ever since the first wrestling practices that season, Hunter had felt in control. In control in every match, even with guys much larger than himself. He was wrestling in groups with the 167 pounders, weighing only 145, a significant difference in the world of grappling. The guy who was the

167 man was good. He was holding his own with him, and even beating him sometimes. It seemed that the guys in his weight class, and weight classes close to his, were no match. He would throw them around, and pin them at will. He was the strongest. He was the fastest. He was unbeatable. He was indestructible . . . or so he thought.

Hunter had become cocky - although it didn't seem so at the time. Success had made him a little too confident, no matter how founded the thoughts were. He would soon learn a very valuable lesson in life. A lesson he didn't fully understand until years later.

His first match, a tournament, was coming up. Hunter knew he would win, he knew he was the best. The first confirmation of this came the week before the tournament. The team had a scrimmage at Columbian High School, where several other area teams met. He rode to the scrimmage with one of the other guys on the team, Rick Tray. Rick was in his weight class, but posed no threat whatsoever. Hunter usually pinned him very quickly, he just wasn't that good. At least compared to "Jambo," he thought.

At the scrimmage, he again proved his dominance. No one posed a challenge, and the coach had actually bumped him up a weight class to try to get some competition. He still seemed to dominate. At the end of the day he was quite confident. He was going to State this year. He knew it.

The tournament was rapidly approaching, and wrestle-offs were set up to see who would be on the varsity line up. Although he knew he would win, he was still very nervous. "What if I screw up and get pinned?" he thought. He would just be sure that didn't happen. He would dominate the two other people in his class, Rick Tray and Rod Henton. He was not worried at all about Rick, but if Rod got you in the right hold it could spell trouble. Rod had a weakness though. At the beginning of this past football season, Rod got his foot caught in a pile up and twisted it backwards breaking the bones. He just wasn't that nimble with it yet. If he had to, Hunter could use it against him.

The time came. The warm up went well, Hunter felt very strong - invincible. The team set up in two circles to commence the test. Each coach, he had two, officiated one of the mats. The first few light guy matches went fast. Hunter's blood was pumping fast, he was ready. All three wrestlers had picked numbers to see who would wrestle first, Rod drew the bye. Rick and Hunter went to the center of the mat.

He could see the fear in his eyes. Hunter knew he was afraid of him because of his physical strength, which fueled his anticipation. All sounds seemed to fade away as the two took positions in the center of the circle, each with a foot on the starting lines opposing one another. Moore, the head coach, was officiating. He put his whistle in his mouth. "Shake Hands," he said in a muffled voice as the whistle blocked the words.

Hunter shook his hand hard, very hard. He knew it hurt his opponent. This was another step in the psychological warfare. Hunter had worked himself into a frenzy; he could feel his body shake with exhilaration. He placed his hands in front of his body. Rick could rarely, if ever, stop him when he went for a take down. Hunter was going to put him away fast. Rick's fear fueled his aggression.

"Ready, Wrestle!" the coach announced.

Hunter immediately shot in for a single leg take down. Rick's defenses were futile. By the time he started to sprawl his legs to the rear, he was well within Hunter's grasp. Hunter reached across to the rear of his opposite knee and pulled up hard. The stunned victim fell directly onto his back. Hunter followed his upper section to the mat, reaching and snagging Rick's upper arm with his left arm, pulling it into his armpit. It was like taking candy from a baby. To add the coup de gras, Hunter ground his chin into Rick's right shoulder. He squeezed everything very hard. The pain that Hunter was inflicting quickly diminished his will to fight, as the coach counted the seconds his shoulder blades were against the mat.

"Fall," the makeshift ref. exclaimed, as he slapped the mat. Hunter released his death grip and helped Rick to his feet. Both men resumed their starting positions, as is customary after a match, and shook hands. "Good match," he assured him. But Rick knew it really wasn't. That was clear. The fear that had dominated his face had turned to anger and frustration. Hunter unsnapped his headgear and strutted off the mat.

Just as he reached the edge of the mat the coach called. "Hunter, I want you to go the whole six minutes." Apparently he wanted Jim to get a little more of a workout before he wrestled Rod. This concerned him. He wanted to be fresh, just in case so he could put Rod away quick too. He would just make sure to conserve his energy with Rick since he wasn't much of a challenge anyway.

Both wrestlers returned to the starting position in the middle. Rick had a different look on his face this time. Anger. It concerned Hunter a little, but he knew there was nothing Rick could do to him. 'I'll just play with him for six minutes, then still be fresh for Rod", he thought.

The commands came again, "Ready, Wrestle!" Hunter shot in again, this time for a fireman's carry. It had much the same result. Rick went down to his back as Hunter covered his body, pinning his shoulder blades to the mat. The coach began to count the back points. When he got to two, Hunter let him up all the way to the standing position. Both circled each other. Hunter went in and locked up, placing his right hand on the back of Rick's neck, his left hand on Rick's elbow. He began squeezing his neck hard, knowing he was inflicting even more pain. All legal, but rough. Hunter quickly pushed Rick's arm skyward and ducked under to a position directly behind him. Hunter picked him up violently, so both of his feet were off the mat and slammed him to the ground, again maneuvering to put him on his back. As the coach reached two, Hunter again let him up. This continued for a third time. Take down, back points, then up. Not only was Rick really getting frustrated, but this humiliating experience was breeding desperation in his eyes. Hunter, feeling as though he was only following the coaches' orders, continued the slaughter.

After Hunter had let him up for the third time Rick was completely desperate. Rick rushed toward him and lunged in for a single leg take down. Hunter lethargically countered and let him pick his right foot up. He was balancing on his left foot, with Rick gripping his right. Rick had his right hand at Hunter's toes and his left at the heel of his shoe. Hunter's first thought was, "I'll go down and work on my escapes. Then he'll feel like he got a take down."

Hunter spun hard to his left and down. At the exact same microsecond, Rick gripped his foot tight with the strength that comes from all consuming anger and twisted the opposite direction. The gates of hell seemed to open and a flood of excruciating pain flowed though Hunter's very being. There were three very loud "POPS" in rapid succession. The torrential wave of instantaneous pain shot up his leg and through his soul. Hunter knew it was broke. "Pain this sharp only comes from a break," he thought. The immense pain began to dull.

"Fuck!" Hunter screamed with the power of man whose very mortality has just come into question. All he could think about was the end of his glorious state-bound year. He could hear Rick go screaming as he ran from the wrestling mat, his voice fading like the hopes of the glory he was to have. Hunter began to lift his head to look over his right shoulder to survey the damage, when Loren Chansoler, the other coach, shoved his face into the mat. Coach Chansoler immediately through a towel over Hunter's head. "You're gonna be OK, just lye still," he assured.

"Is it broke coach?" Hunter asked.

"You're gonna be all right, just lie still" he reiterated.

Hunter buried his face in the mat. The pain dulled more, and almost turning into a numbness. "I won't go to state, I won't go to state now!" went over and over in his mind. Hunter asked several more times if his leg was broke. Each time receiving the same reassurances about being "OK." It was obvious it was broke, but no one wanted to say that to Hunter.

Before Hunter knew it he heard the voices of his dad, mom, and sister. The first thing that he could make out came from his sister; "Is his foot suppose to look like that?"

The statement confirmed that there was something seriously wrong. Hunter figured that his leg was broke in half and was at some weird angle off to the side. The ambulance arrived at about the same time, and the EMT's put him on a gurney.

At the hospital everyone was a buzz. Hunter was only in the emergency room for a few minutes when someone directed an orderly to wheel him down to X-ray. Each time Hunter managed to look up at anyone, he was always greeted with same look of concern. "How bad is it?" he wondered. An orderly who looked like Jerry Garcia from the Grateful Dead was tasked to transport him. The orderly was slightly overweight with long hair that had been pulled back into a ponytail, thick square glasses, and a slightly overgrown beard to top it off. He started some senseless conversation about how his day was going when Hunter broke in. "Hey man, is my leg bent in half or what? Nobody will tell me anything."

The response was very descriptive. "Dude. Your leg is twisted completely backwards man. I've never seen anything this bad before!"

Hunter's head dropped into the pillow.

When Hunter returned from X-ray, the bone specialist was there. "My name is Doctor Zender," he stated in a heavy accent. He was very dark complexioned, Hunter guessed that he must be from Pakistan or India. Hunter couldn't see anything, but could feel the touch of the doctor surveying his leg. He could hear the doctor talking to his parents in an urgent voice, indiscernible to Hunter because of the doctor's thick accent.

"We must turn his foot back around now. There is no blood flow to the foot, and if we don't do it now, he could lose his foot." His words were very rushed with a hint of panic in them.

"Can't you give him something for the pain?" Hunter's father asked.

Up to this point they hadn't given him anything for the pain.

"We don't have time," the doctor replied.

Hunter's dad came to his side. "They're going to have to turn your foot back around." The fear and apprehension chiseled on his face. He grabbed Hunter's hand, "Just squeeze my hand when it hurts."

Hunter could feel the doctor positioning himself on the deformed foot. A wave of nausea flew through his system.

"OK, here we go," the doctor announced.

The pain was like an incredible blinding light that permeated through every pour in Hunter's body. Hunter screamed from the bottom of his soul, and squeezed his father's hand so tight that he was surprised he didn't break it.

Then there was an overwhelming wave of relief. It was as though a thousand pound weight had been lifted from his chest. An angelical rush of reprieve covered his body.

The ominous tune brought him back into the aircraft.
"This will be the day that I die," *I wish the song would stop.*
Hunter had been on the aircraft for almost eight hours. The combat gear he wore weighted down every part of his body. He had two drums of SAW (Squad Automatic Weapon) ammo, one on either side. Four grenades. "Were all my pins taped down?" he thought. *Yes, they were,* he was sure. What if one gets hooked on someone's gear and gets pulled? They won't; He was sure he had faced the pins to the inside of the ammo case. Six 30-round magazines of 5.56. Hunter's SAW was firmly in his 1950 case along his side. In his ruck, Hunter had the essential gear he needed and his demo with his blasting caps in his left front breast pocket of his BDU top. Hunter loved blowing things up ever since demolition school; the power was awesome. He was to blow up the communication tower at Dog, his squad's first objective. "That should be awesome," he thought, "I hope I make it there."

As he looked around, he saw that many of the Rangers were asleep. Heads bobbing with the motion of the aircraft, many with their faces pointing skyward as they slept. It had often amazed Hunter how Rangers could sleep in the strangest places, under the strangest circumstances, many knowing that these could be the last hours of their lives.

The cabin of the aircraft was dimly lit, packed front to back with jumpers. In the center of the aircraft was a divider that ran the length of the cargo area, seats constructed of tubing and orange straps protruding from either side. Another set of seats were positioned on the outer walls of the plane, facing inward. It made a pretty neat set up; two rows of jumpers facing each other on each side of the airplane. The entire capacity of the cargo hold was utilized, 64 jumpers all packed together so tight it was hard to tell where one person and his gear ended and another started. Some people had elected to keep their Kevlar helmets on as they slept, for added padding, most of the others placed this vital piece of equipment on their large rucksacks, positioned squarely on their laps. Everyone's faces were painted with dark paint in the traditional Ranger tiger pattern, which served to disguise their features so well on some individuals that the only thing that could be made out was the whiteness of their eyes. Hunter was one of these individuals. The paint covered every part of his face, eyebrows, eyelids, lips, ears, and even extended well up onto his shaved head.

CHAPTER 2

Hunter had even shaved his head in school. It seemed that there were a lot of really great times back in high school. The incredible feeling of being the hero. Everybody knows your name. Everybody wants to talk to you. Everybody smiles. It's that feeling that everything is right in the world. Jim could vividly remember the day he had first felt that way. As he closed his eyes he could picture it all. Everything from that night, every sound, every smell, every picture. . .

He could hear the drums. Boom, Boom, Clap...Boom, Boom, Clap. The adrenaline was flowing. It was fourth down at Warrior Field on the third game of his sophomore year, and it was time to fly down the field. Hunter could distinctly hear the song "We will Rock you" by Queen in his head.

Hunter was the right end on the punt team. All he had to do was wait until the ball was snapped, streak down the field as fast as he could and tackle the guy returning the punt. He loved it. If Jim could get through the defensive line quickly, he usually had a pretty clear shot at the guy returning the ball. The best part was that he could usually be at almost full speed when he hit the guy, if he didn't allude him.

"Set," the up back barked out the signs. "Hut, Hut, HUT!"

Hunter got off the line very quickly, barely brushing the defender across from him. Jim accelerated to top speed, feeling as if he was floating down the field on a rocket. When he was at complete top speed, he always felt as if only his toes hit the ground instead of his whole feet. This was one of those times.

It was as though everything went into slow motion. There were two people directly in front of the punt return man. The one in front was in a stationary position watching Hunter, the other tracking a different pursuer. Just behind the blockers was the ball returner, his eyes gazing into the sky tracking the football as it floated down to him from the heavens. As Hunter approached, the brown streak of the ball came into view as it descended toward earth. The blocker was now ten yards directly in front of him.

Within fifteen yards, it must have been apparent to the blocker that he would have to engage, as Hunter was the first one downfield. The blocker's anticipating eyes focused on Hunter. Just behind him the ball reached the returner, catching it with both arms in front of his body. His opponent turned his head to the open side of the field, Hunter's side. As he took his first lateral step, Hunter only adjusted his course slightly to the open side of the field. The blocker remained stationary, not able to see the lateral movement of his teammate behind him. Jim was within five yards now at full speed. The center of his facemask, forming a sort of cross hairs, seemed to lock onto the ball carriers. As he took a stride, exposing his open chest, Hunter hit him. He hadn't lost any momentum, the impact was incredible. He could feel his entire power surge through his opponent like a projectile. The ball returner's body folded under the incredible pressure and flew backwards. The football flew from his arms. Hunter scurried off the fallen player to recover the football.

The crowd went crazy, the sound of cheers were explosive. Then he heard it, first as a low pounding chant, then into a monstrous roar; "HUN-TER, HUN-TER, HUN-TER."

Another sharp jolt of turbulence brought Jim back to reality. "Ok, Ok, am I forgetting anything?" He began to run through his mental checklist.

Along with his standard sticks of C-4 explosive, he had rigged two in case he encountered one of the KM900 armored personal carriers that might be on the objective. "KM900's", he thought, "That's like an armored car with machine guns and bullet proof tires on it." He wondered why he had never seen or heard about them down here when he spent a month in Jungle School. He had put a six second fuse on two of the demolition sticks and had made sure that the backing for the pressure tape would come off easily. He had a few extra grenades in the outside pockets of his ruck, just in case. On the very top he had a LAW rocket secured under the top flap. The LAW was basically a shoulder fired anti-tank rocket, but Hunter had learned in Special OP's that they could be used for many different things. The whole ruck weighed over 80 pounds. That's all right he thought, he was used to it.

An incredible burning pressure was growing. "I have to pee so bad I can taste it!" he thought. The Rangers were packed in the aircraft so tight that the only thing he could move was his head. He had to go bad! Several people had been walking across the human road of rucksacks to the front of the aircraft to go, and Hunter had seen a piss bucket. He could hardly wait, it felt like his bladder was going to explode. Wouldn't that be a funny thing, he though, die because he had to pee before he even got out of the aircraft. The bucket was just across the inboard side of aircraft when he spotted it. Hunter woke the man across from him and asked him if he could reach the crew chief just behind him that had it. He signaled with his hand and the bucket was passed to Hunter's eager hands.

Hunter struggled to stand on the seat, banging into both guys on either side of him. He unhooked one side of the strap holding his ruck to his D-ring, part of his parachute harness attached to his body, to clear the way. When he finally went, it was as though the pressure of the world lifted from his body. A tremendous surge of relief ran over him, creating an almost euphoric state. *Thank God.* Hunter handed it again to the guy across from him to be passed forward. He then hooked his ruck back up. "I hooked everything up right, right?," he thought. *I did, I think, I'm sure.* Hunter wiggled back into his sandwiched seat. "This will be the day that I die, this will be the day that I die. Those good old boys were drinking whiskey and rye."

Hunter could see that some information was being passed back through the stick (the line of jumpers) and could hear bits and pieces over the whine of the engines as it got closer. "They ..n't kn.. were co..n," to the next man, then to the guy on his left. The Ranger next to him turned to Hunter and shouted over the noise with a smile, "They don't know we're coming." Hunter could feel a surge of adrenaline shoot through his veins. "Hooah, yea baby." He turned and repeated the message down the line.

I wonder if the SEAL team was on the beach? Hunter thought. How many of those PDF bastards would those 2000-pound bombs kill? Will God punish me for killing? He shouldn't; I'm doing my job to protect my country. I'm going to kick some ass. When was the last time I said, "I love you to my family?" They must know I love them. I wish I had been more productive in this life. I wish I would have had a kid. I will make my family and country proud. I will give my life for my country. I will bring honor to my family and my name. I really hope I can die in a blaze of glory, so they can be proud. I hope they know I love them.

As Hunter looked to his left he could see an officer standing in front of the stick. He must be the jumpmaster, he thought. Hunter could see his lips move, and recognized the sign, twenty minutes. The words were transferred from person to person back the stick. Since Hunter was about half way back, it made its way to him quickly. Hunter didn't know the guy next to him. *He must be from Charlie Company* Hunter thought, he could see his squad leader a few people up from his spot. "Twenty minutes," the guy next to Hunter shouted as he turned his head. In turn, Hunter looked to his right and shouted the warning to the next person. The jump commands would come soon. They were to start six minutes before the jump, but inevitably the time between twenty and six always turned out to be about five minutes max. Hunter could feel the surge through his body. Something James had said to him just before they boarded the aircraft hit him, "I'll see you on the ground, whoba." He always said whoba, instead of hooah- - it was his thing. James was a good guy. "If I make it to the ground . . . I don't want to die in the air," Hunter thought.

Hunter's path through the military to this point was definitely eventful. He had been tested many times, always meeting the challenge.

Hunter wondered; *how many people know the feeling? The feeling of absolute strength, absolute confidence, and absolute dedication.* Not many he guessed.

To know that you are the best, in a group of the best, hand selected. Selected because you are the strongest, the fastest, the smartest, the most dangerous. Special Operations is a unique thing. Its purpose is different from other forms of the military, thus the training, the methods, and the mentality is different.

People would ask Hunter, "why do they do that to those guys?" In reference to their training and their lifestyle. Hunter would always point out two things; they volunteered to do these things of their own free will, and the things they must do require these methods. To go to war you must become war. Hunter had been through some of the most rigorous training in the military, training that some would consider hell, and now it was time to use it.

CHAPTER 3

Hunter remembered when he first went to the Ranger Indoctrination Program, RIP for short. The Ranger Sergeant that had picked Hunter's group up after completing Airborne school seemed quite somber, but Hunter could tell it was an act. He stood by the door of the military bus in the parking lot with a clipboard. As men moved toward the bus, he would casually ask; "You going to RIP? This is the bus. Get on with your gear." He was almost cordial. He was too mellow.

Hunter stated his name as he entered the bus. "Private Hunter, Sergeant."

Soon the bus was almost jammed packed, everyone with his duffel bag full of gear. As the last entered the bus, the Ranger jumped in and closed the door. He nodded to the driver and the bus moved. The RIP compound was located about a mile away from Airborne School, in some old World War II barracks overlooking the airfield. The Ranger remained silent, never looking back at the men on the bus. There was an ominous silence throughout all the people in the passenger seats. It reminded Hunter of the calm before the storm. The bus pulled up in front of the barracks and stopped. Then hell broke loose.

When the Ranger turned around, there was pure hatred on his face. "I'm going to give you one minute to be off this bus and in a formation in front of this building." It was a very calm, deliberate statement.

There was a mad rush to get off the bus everyone pushing for the door and people flying out the door as they got there. Hunter was toward the back of the bus, and he knew he was going to get smoked.

"GET THE FUCK OFF THE BUS, NOW!" another cadre screamed from outside. When Hunter reached the bus door, he leaped over the steps to the ground and scrambled toward the formation. Everyone was already in the front leaning rest position. Hunter took a place in one of the last rows and immediately went into the push up position.

"This is a team. If one fails you all fail. If you fail people die. Your Ranger buddy dies. You fail to complete the mission." The Ranger barked. "In cadence. . ." He also went to the front leaning rest position.

"In cadence," every one repeated.

"Begin. One, two, three," the Ranger begin to call the repletion, doing the push ups with the group.

"One!" The entire group repeated.

This continued until the count reached 100 repetitions. Push-ups were always Hunters strong point, so he had no problem keeping pace. Almost everyone else had their butts high in the air in a resting position by the end.

"Recover!" The instructor announced.

Everyone stood to the ridged position of attention.

"You will have the opportunity to quit this program at any time. You do not need to feel ashamed. You will be assigned to a regular army unit. Does any one want to quit?" he asked.

No one made a sound or moved.

"If you fail any part of this selection course, you will be dropped. If you fall back on any run, you will be dropped. If you fall back on any road march, you will be dropped. If you fail any of the tests in this course, you will be dropped. Do you understand me?" he continued.

"Yes Sergeant!" the mass of voices replied.

"The side straddle hop," he announced. This was what the army called jumping jacks.

"The side straddle hop!" everyone repeated.

"Begin. One, two, three,"

"ONE!" the group echoed.

This continued until 250, the Ranger sergeant doing every rep with the group.

"There is no room for weakness in the BAT," the Ranger announced, seemingly not even sweating from the physical exertion. "Weakness leads to death on the battlefield. If you die, your Ranger buddy dies, and you fail to complete the mission. Most of you standing here now will not complete this course. You should feel no shame in that. The BAT requires only the best. Failure here only means you will be assigned to a regular unit. Failure on the battlefield means death. Does anyone want to quit?"

Again no one moved.

"You soon will," he responded. "On your back, MOVE!"

The group instantaneously flew to the ground.

"Flutter kicks, start position, MOVE!"

Everyone raised their feet six inches off the ground, and prepared to move their feet up and down, with their hands at their sides. Everyone started the cadence of the repetitions again, and this time went to 250. Most could not handle the pace. Hunter found it excruciating, but he loved it. The adrenalin flowing through his veins wasn't just from the exercise, it was from the challenge. Looking around the group, he could see that the strain from the exercise was getting to most of the group. They would go as far as their body, or mind, would let them. They would then stop the exercise with the onslaught of exhaustion. As the pain would increase Hunter would think about his family and all the support they had shown him as he grew up. He would also think about those naysayers, whom he had worked with while waiting to get into the military. Several people he worked with had said he would never make it when he had told them what he was going to do. Their voices echoed in his head as the pain increased, there was no way he was going to let them be right. He would finish, he would make it, he would succeed. Hunter had made a promise to himself, he would make it or he would die trying.

As the mass of individuals finished an exercise, the instructor would stand and ask if there was anyone who wanted to quit. This went on for what seemed to be hours. At the end there were several people who had quit. The group then went to another building to be issued their gear for the course.

The formation was much larger than the men who were on the bus. It seemed that there were many who were already there. After several smoke sessions (hard PT workouts), everyone was taken into the barracks and told to find a bunk. Hunter chose one about five bunks from the door and threw his duffel bag on it. Just as he sat down, one of the other students came running through the door. "Formation! Formation!" he shouted

Everyone sprinted for the door and into the formation area.

"What in the fuck took you so long Rangers?" one of the cadre exclaimed. "If one fails you all fail. You are only as fast as your slowest man! Front leaning rest position, MOVE!"

Everyone dropped to the push up position. The Ranger cadre went down also. The formation counted cadence for another 75 push-ups.

"You are being released for the evening. You will have all your gear properly laid out, as per SOP, for inspection after PT tomorrow morning. You will be standing tall in formation for PT at 04:30. Is that clear?" he stated.

The answer was also in unison, "Yes Sergeant!"

"Dismissed!"

Everyone shot back to the barracks. Inside they all started laying out their gear exactly like the SOP chart in everyone's wall locker showed. The entire process of properly laying out the equipment took several hours. After Hunter had completed his display, he headed to the latrine to take a shower.

The latrine (bathroom) was typical for the World War II barracks. There were five toilets sitting two feet apart against the wall. This was very interesting when they were in use as one person's knees would hit their buddy if you both were going to the bathroom at the same time. The showers were small with several water heads. A major obstacle was the water temperature and pressure. If someone flushed the toilet when someone was in the shower, the water pressure would be cut in half and the temperature would become scalding. For this reason, anytime someone was about to flush the toilet they would have to scream "Flush" to notify anyone in harm's way.

After a shower, Hunter put on his PT gear, the gray army shorts and shirt, and went to sleep in his bunk.

Hunter's watch alarm went off at 04:00 just as he had set it. As he rose, several people were moving about the open bay. Hunter grabbed his toothbrush, and headed for the latrine. After finishing his business in there he drank a full canteen of water in anticipation of the heavy workouts that would be taking place during the day. A curiously nervous expectation surged through his body, almost like a rush of adrenaline. He was ready.

Hunter headed out the door into the formation area that was lit by pole lights with all the others at 04:20. They lined up in one large mass formation, and stood silently at attention. The seconds creeped by, as a glow and faint laughter radiated from the CP building 50 meters to their front left. Soon the door to the structure swung open, and several Ranger cadre exited with their black PT gear on.

One Ranger instructor moved to the front of the formation, just in front of the class leader who was centered on the group. The day before they had been divided up in squads, and a class leader and squad leaders were chosen at random. It was each squad leader's responsibility to keep track of all the people in his squad. Which, in a group this large, meant just making sure there were the right number of people there.

"PLATOON, ATTENTION!" The class leader shouted vigorously, which didn't facilitate any movement because everyone was already was at attention. He then saluted the Cadre and announced; "Sergeant, class is formed."

The instructor returned the salute. "Class leader, How many Rangers are in the formation?"

The class leader hesitated. "One hundred fifty.....four, Sergeant!"

The Ranger instructors face transformed instantly to a mask of disgust. The veins in his neck began to protrude from the skin, appearing to engorge with some inner rage that was bursting to get out. The sharp features of his jaw line became more pronounced.

"ARE YOU SURE CLASS LEADER?" the instructor asked.

"NO, SERGEANT!" he responded.

"So what you're telling me is that one, or some of your men could be AWOL?"

"NO, SERGEANT!" the class leader again replied.

"HOW IN THE FUCK DO YOU KNOW THAT, IF YOU DON'T KNOW HOW MANY MEN YOU ARE SUPPOSE TO HAVE STANDING IN FORMATION?" the Ranger persisted.

"I DON"T KN. . ." he tried to finish before being cut off in mid sentence.

"YOU HAVE FAILED TO MAINTAIN ACCOUNTABILITY OF YOUR MEN. A RANGER ALWAYS HAS ACCOUNTABILITY OF HIS MEN AND EQUIPMENT. YOU HAVE FAILED TO DO THIS! WHEN A RANGER FUCKS UP PEOPLE DIE ON THE BATTLEFIELD. YOU ARE RELIEVED OF COMMAND." the instructor continued. "FALL IN AT THE END OF FIRST SQUAD!"

"YES SERGEANT!" he vigorously replied, and then ran to the end of first squad and resumed the position of attention.

The instructor looked down at his clipboard. "RANGER BRUNO!"

"HERE SERGEANT!" Bruno sounded off from the second row of people.

"POST!" the Ranger ordered.

Bruno ran down the row of people in his squad then around to the front of the formation screaming loudly like a wild man as he went. When he was directly in front of the instructor he came to the position of attention and saluted; "RANGER BRUNO REPORTING AS ORDERED, SERGEANT!"

"VERY GOOD RANGER BRUNO. I HAD BETTER SEE THE SAME KIND OF MOTIVATION FROM THE REST OF YOU. RANGER BRUNO, YOUR ARE NOW CLASS LEADER. YOU HAVE ONE HUNDRED AND FIFTY SIX RANGERS IN YOUR CLASS. IS THAT CLEAR?"

"YES, SERGEANT!" Bruno replied.

"RANGERS, IT IS NOW TIME FOR ROLE CALL. SOUND OFF WHEN YOUR NAME IS CALLED!" The instructor barked.

"ABERNATHY," he started at the beginning of the alphabetical list.

"HERE, SERGEANT!" Abernathy replied.

This continued through the entire list of people. When Hunter's name was announced he sounded off with the loudest most concise annunciation possible.

Soon the instructor had finished the entire list. "OPEN RANKS, MARCH!"

This was how PT always started in the Army. Basically the entire formation spreads out. When there are four ranks (rows), the first takes one step forward, the second remains in place, the third takes two steps to the rear (which is equal to one forward because they are much shorter), and the third takes four to the rear. Everyone began with stretching. Then came the brutal physical exertion. Literally hundreds of pushups, sit-ups, crunches, side straddle hops, etcetera. Hunter loved it. He could feel the pain of the weak in the group and it made him stronger. Every single Ranger instructor did every rep of every exercise with the candidates.

After they finished, the instructor ordered the group to close ranks, and then began to speak. "THERE IS NO ROOM IN A RANGER BATALLION FOR WEAKNESS. WITH THE THINGS WE DO, A WEAK LINK MEANS DEATH AND FAILURE TO COMPLETE THE MISSION. SERGEANT PALATO, WHAT IS THE LAST STANZA OF THE RANGER CREED?".

One of the other instructors, who was standing toward the rear of the formation sounded off. "READILY WILL I DISPLAY THE INTESTINAL FORTITUDE REQUIRED TO FIGHT ON TO THE RANGER OBJECTIVE AND COMPLETE THE MISSION, THOUGH I BE THE LONE SURVIVOR!"

The Ranger instructor continued; "THERE ARE ONLY TWO TIMES A RANGER EVER QUITS. WHEN THE MISSION HAS BEEN COMPLETED, OR WHEN HE IS DEAD. THERE ARE NO EXCEPTIONS. THIS IS NOT A PLACE FOR THE WEAK. THERE IS NO SHAME IN QUITTING THIS COURSE, GENTLEMEN. IT DOES NOT MEAN YOU ARE A FAILURE, IT MEANS THAT YOU JUST HAVE FAILED AT THIS TIME TO MEET THE CRITERIA REQUIRED TO BE A RANGER. DOES ANYONE WANT TO QUIT?"

Several people raised their hands.

"OK, THOSE OF YOU WHO DO NOT WANT TO CONTINUE THIS COURSE WILL BREAK RANKS AND REPORT OVER TO THE CP."

The people who had quit stepped out of the rank they were in and ran over to the CP.

"THE REST OF YOU BETTER BE PREPARED TO GO THROUGH HELL. TODAY WE WILL RUN UNTIL 30 OF YOU FALL OUT. IT MIGHT BE FIVE MILES, IT MIGHT BE TWENTY. IF YOU FALL BACK, OR OUT , ON THIS RUN YOU WILL BE DROPPED FROM THIS COURSE.

DOES ANYONE WANT TO QUIT NOW AND SAVE YOUR SELF THE AGONY?"

No one else raised their hand.

The RIP compound was poised on top of a large hill overlooking a large valley where the airfield was. Hunter figured they would start fast just to mind fuck a lot of guys, they did. They briskly jogged to the top of the hill and then down. At the bottom the instructor began the sprint. The Ranger Sergeant started the pace at a 6-minute mile, and guys in the class began to fall. With every one that fell back, Hunter became stronger, more motivated, more determined. They only ran seven miles on that outing, at the end sprinting up the hill (known as cardiac hill). By the end of the day, they had dropped forty people.

CHAPTER 4

After completing the course, Hunter's first experience in his Ranger Battalion was very interesting. They put the group assigned to 3rd Battalion in a room on the first floor of the Alpha Company barracks. A sergeant had picked the group up at the old World War II reception barracks they were staying in, and marched them the mile to the compound. Upon entering the Alpha Company barracks, he directed the group into the day room and put them at parade rest. No one had spoken since they had been directed to get their gear and get into formation for the trip to the BAT (the slang term for "the Ranger Battalion)".

A short stocky sergeant entered the room after a few minutes. He started at one end of the line of Rangers that wrapped around the room, looking over each private from head to toe.

He stopped in front of Hunter, looking him up and down. Hunter kept his icy stare straight ahead.

"Ranger Hunter, what is your PT score?" he yelled into his face. His lower lip filled with tobacco. The smell was rancid. His eyes only inches from Hunter's nose.

"299 Sergeant!" Hunter shouted back. A perfect score was 300, and he thought that would impress him. Hunter didn't know what to think. *Was this my future squad leader? Should I try to impress him?* He had no idea what was going on.

He moved to Hunter's side, facing him, again looking Hunter up and down. He wrapped his hands around his neck, as to measure the size. "Do you lift weights Ranger?" he asked.

"Roger Sergeant!" Hunter barked back.

He put his hands around the top part of Hunters arm to measure, much as he did his neck.

"How much do you bench press Ranger?" he continued.

"About 400 pounds Sergeant!" Hunter responded.

Moving again to his front, he put one hand on either side of Hunter's midsection, then his stomach area, then hips. He pushed on each hip from the side, as to test the stability. It reminded him of a farmer checking out some livestock before buying it.

"Do you like to fight Ranger?" he asked.

"Roger, I love to fight Sergeant!"

Then he measured the tops of Hunter's legs. First the size, then moving them to apparently test the joints. Then the calves, moving the lower leg to test the knee. He then moved to the other side and repeated the process.

Hunter remained at a ridged parade rest position, with his back straight, hands crossed at the small of the back, legs spread shoulder with, staring straight ahead.

When the Ranger Sergeant had completed his survey, he returned to a position directly in front of Hunter. "Let me see your war face Ranger," he commanded.

Hunter scowled with the meanest face he knew and screamed at the top of his lungs. He could feel his neck strain, his whole body flexing with exertion.

"When you see the First Sergeant, you tell him you want to come to first platoon, first squad. You got me Ranger!" he barked, again just inches from Hunter's face.

"Roger, Sergeant!" Hunter responded.

"First platoon, First squad!" he continued

"Roger Sergeant, First platoon, first squad!"

CHAPTER 5

Emil Rojo Rodriguez had been put on security patrol for the base at Rio Hato. He normally didn't mind the duty, in fact he was honored that he was trusted enough to help secure and protect the very place that El Presidente currently occupied.

Most people didn't know when El Presidente was on the post, even the elite Special Forces troops, that Emil was a member of. Occasionally when they were here in garrison, one of Emil's comrades would see the motorcade and alert the rest of the unit of their "special visitor." El Presidente's beach house was located on the West end of the compound, facing the Ocean, so he often graced the post with presence - even if his presence was secret.

Emil gripped the pistol grip of his AK-74 assault rifle. It gave him a sense of pride, of belonging, of power. He had learned to use guns very early in his life on the streets of Colon.

His father had left his mother when he was only three years old. Emil and his mother were forced to scrounge and beg for food while living in a cardboard and tin shack on the outskirts of town. He joined a local street gang when he was ten and vowed to have vengeance on that "pig" that left his mother in such a terrible state. By the time he was sixteen he ran the gang. And so it came to pass that he developed a warranted reputation as a particularly cruel individual in his day-to-day muggings until the day he found his father and graduated to murderer.

Emil remembered the day well, the day he brought his vengeance to bare on the man that had left him and his mother in that hell hole to die. He had often fantasized about what he would do to the man, and many times as he beat someone who questioned his growing authority – or one of his many victims, he would picture the face in the old black and white picture that his mother had given him. For some pathetic reason she did not blame her husband for leaving. But Emil had no sympathy, in fact he didn't feel anything for others except for spite and hate. Had a Psychiatrist evaluated Emil it would have been very clear that he had developed into a sadistic psychopath.

One rainy day on the outskirts of Colon, Emil had decided to wander into one of the local bars that he often frequented to get a drink and partake in one of the women that he prostituted. As he entered the door with two of his closest "advisors", he immediately noticed that something was different. Very rarely would anyone but the locals even think about going into such an establishment that had clearly been marked by the painted graffiti on the outside wall as Emil's gang. But there sat a man at the end of the bar that was clearly new. The man sat half hunched over his cerveza on the bar, perched on one of the wooden bar stools – staring up at a black and white television above the bar. He wore a rather large floppy straw hat that looked as though it had the dirt of ten years ground into the weave.

Emil walked up next to individual and leaned on the bar, he sharply reached up and flicked the hat from the man's head. "What are you doing in here punta?" he asked.

The man's eyes flicked in terror as he cowered and looked at the wiry Emil hovering above him, "Nothing Sir. . . Nothing at. . . I just"

As the man's terrified gaze peered up at him, the light of recognition filled Emil's face. A smile danced on his lips. "Lois, Lois Rodriguize!"

The man's haggard face drew blank, "Ah, ah, yes, yes. . . how do you know my name?"

Emil gestured to the bartender, raising his hand high and letting out a shrill whistle. "Two whiskeys. Oh I know you well my friend – In fact, we will celebrate our reunion."

"Reunion? But Sir. . ." the man stumbled over the words. He stared at Emil trying to place the face."

"Do I not look familiar old man?" Emil grabbed the man's greasy hair and thrust his face into his own, holding it only inches away. "Do I not look familiar?" He screamed, rancid spit laden with tobacco juice splattering Lois's face. "MAYBE MY NAME WILL HELP, EMIL ROJO RODRIGUEZ!"

The old man's mouth opened in disbelief. "No, it can't be – Emil . . . my son? You . . . you have".

"Grown? Yes I have – no thanks to you pig," the spit again splattering with the final word. A large grin again possessed Emil's face as two whiskeys were placed in front of them. "Drink up my wayward father. You have a very long night ahead of you.

The man took the whisky with trembling hands. "Emil, I only".

"Shut up pig," Emil shot back "the only sounds I want to hear from you are your screams as you are slaughtered like the pig you are."

Lois broke into a low uncontrolled sob, "but I never meant to".

"Shut up pig." Emil grabbed the back of his hair again and drew his face close once again, smiling all the while, "I said shut up pig. You will need all your strength."

Emil slowly drew his face away and turned his father's head in the original direction he had been facing when he had entered the bar. "Drink your whisky and cerveza." He slammed his head forward hitting the half filled glass of beer, kicking it off the back of the bar as Lois's head impacted the bar with great force. Both men who had entered with Emil laughed.

"I guess you can't drink your cerveza since you have spilled it, so you better drink your whisky.

Lois's eyebrow dripped blood from where his head had hit the glass. "Please, please, Emil, I . . ."

Emil smashed his right elbow into his mouth knocking him off the chair. Blood began to poor out of a large gash from the inside Lois's mouth as Emil's two men helped him to his feet.

"Unless you want me to castrate you here, in front of all of these beautiful ladies", Emil gestured to the three prostitutes at the opposite end of the bar, "I suggest you . . . shut . . . the . . . fuck . . . up."

Emil sat down on a bar stool and drank his whisky as his men held Lois, his body slumped over in a gesture of resignation. When Emil had downed his whisky, he turned to Lois again. "I think you should have some time to think about what you did to your wife and baby son, maybe even repent for your sins. I think you need that – the time – I have had to go through eighteen years of hell, you should at least have a few hours to think about it before I butcher you like a pig."

Lois's head still hung, not looking at Emil. Emil stepped forward and pulled it up so he was once again face to face with the man. "Do you hear me old man? I am going to castrate and slaughter you like a pig."

Emil looked to the man holding Lois's right arm, "Take him to the hut in the jungle. Tie him to the ground so that his feet are in the cutter ant trail – when the ants have eaten away his feet, make sure to put a tourniquet on his lower legs so he doesn't bleed to death. Also start a hot fire for the branding iron. Do you understand? Do not let him bleed to death under any circumstances."

The man nodded in understanding and they dragged Lois out the door and into the street.

When he arrived at the shack in the jungle two hours later, Emil could already hear the muffled screams as he approached and smell the roaring fire that was burning.

Manual and Diego had Lois tied to the ground by ropes attached to the base of four trees. Each rope was tied to one of Lois's limbs. He was staked down in such a way that his ankles crossed a barren path cut through the jungle by voracious ants. Cutter ants cut their way through the jungle, devouring anything in their path. It didn't matter what it was, vegetation or a fallen tree, if it was in the path. Within hours the area where the object blocked the path would be gone. Almost as if someone had cut the object with a saw, which was exactly what was happening to an area of flesh about four inches wide a few inches above Lois's ankles. The ants had already eaten away a large portion of the flesh where some of the bone was exposed on both legs. Manual had tied tourniquets midway up the calf with a rope on both legs to ensure that Lois would not bleed to death.

Lois was floundering against the ropes wildly as Emil approached, screaming a hoarse scream of a man who had been already screaming for hours.

Emil walked up next to the massive wounds on Lois's legs. "I see you are having fun with Manual and Diego my father." He leaned forward, placing his boot on one of the bloody gashes and began to push – grinding his boot in the open flesh. "I don't think you will be leaving your wife and baby to die in a piss hole any more, will you?"

Lois screamed an octave higher with the increased pressure on what was left of his leg. The intense pain was too much and his head fell back, passing out momentarily.

Emil immediately fell to his knees beside his father's head and began slapping him across his face. "Oh no you bastard, no passing out!" Lois came too.

"Get him up." Emil ordered as he began to move to the fire built in front of the sheet metal shack. On one side of the fire protruded a length of steel rod, its end glowing red with white hot heat. "It's time for papa to really get a taste of what he has done."

Emil's two henchmen cut the rope that held Lois to the ground and drug him to the fire as he continued to scream.

Emil entered the rusty shack and emerged a few minutes later holding a large butcher's knife in one hand and an axe in the other. "I have been waiting for this day for a long time." The smile on his face beamed in the mid-afternoon sun. "Remember when I said I was going to butcher you like the pig you are, it's time. Tie his hands and knees."

Manual and Diego held Lois down a few feet from the fire tying his hands behind his back and his knees together. The screams softened to a whimper.

"Lesson number one, never run away from your family," Emil hissed as walked beside Lois's knees. With one swift motion the axe was raised and slammed down – severing one of Lois's feet.

Lois's scream seemed to echo through the jungle. Emil picked up the severed limb and moved to Lois's face. He thrust the foot in Lois's distorted face. "Never run away from your family," he politely repeated.

"Stick his feet in the fire to sear the wounds", he ordered.

Within seconds Manual and Diego had held the bloody stump and the other intact foot in the fire for several seconds, the putrid stench of burning flesh pierced the air. Lois went limp as he passed out for the second time.

"Is he dead?" Diego asked.

"No, he's just napping," Emil responded with a chuckle.

"Manual. Get me a bucket of water," Emil ordered

A minute later Manual returned with a rusty pail of water.

"Throw it on his face," Emil gestured to Lois.

Manual tipped the bucket over Lois's face and poured out the contents. "Wake up sleeping beauty," He mused as the water startled Lois to consciousness.

"No, no, please," Lois begged.

"Oh no, you have more lessons to learn." Emil tossed the severed foot into the fire. "Lesson number two, don't get a woman pregnant if you are not going to take care of her and the child. Get his clothes off and hold his legs open."

Manual and Diego both drew knives and cut the clothes from Lois's body, leaving only the charred remains of pants over his lower calves, the bloody charred remains of what used to be his feet.

"Spread his legs apart," Emil ordered as he removed the white hot rod from the fire.

Manual cut the rope holding Lois's knees together. Lois began to scream at the top of his lungs. "NO, NO, NO," he repeated.

Emil drew his knife close to Lois's testicles and with a smile flicked the knife, slicing open his scrotum. Lois screamed uncontrollably. Then he finished the job by slicing out both testicles.

The blood flowed from between his legs as Lois once again passed out. Emil quickly brought the white hot iron between his legs to sear the wound and slow the bleeding. Lois awoke again but this time didn't scream, just began to shake. "Bring me the duct tape from the house," Emil ordered.

A minute later Manual returned with the tape. Emil scooped up the two bloody testicals from between Lois's legs and grasped Lois's face. Lois's eyes rolled back in his head, only to focus on Emil momentarily and roll back again. Emil forced Lois's mouth open and shoved the testicals inside, then taped his mouth shut.

Lois gagged violently.

With a slight smile on his face, Emil watched as his father choked to death.

Emil would later join the "Macho de Madres" where his special skills would be very useful in dealing with the enemies of El Presidente.

CHAPTER 6

Hunter reviewed the plan in his head. When he got out of the aircraft, he was to locate the runway; it faced east and west. Hunter's objective was on the north side, so if he landed on the South side, "This will be the day that I die, this will be the day that I die" he would have to cross the runway to get to Dog. *That fucking song - - what was the name? Running password is "bulldog." I wonder if that stealth fighter can drop those bombs on the barracks. The SEAL team hits the beach at H minus ten, takes out everybody in the beach house, and gets Noriega in the water by H minus 2. The stealth fighter flies up the coast, drops the bombs on the PDF Special Forces barracks. Then the C130 Specter gun ships start hitting targets with their 105's. Fuck, I hope they kill those fuckin' ZSU 23-4's, I don't want to die in the aircraft. Then we come in low off the sea, jump up to 500 feet and jump.* 500 feet, Hunter wondered why the hell they were even wearing these reserves. They didn't work that low. *That's OK,* he thought, *I want to get to the ground as quick as possible. I know if I make it to the ground, I'll make it to my objective.*

Am I ready to die? I don't know. "This will be the day that I die, this will be the day that I die." *Do they know I love them? I wish I would have had a kid. Anyway, when we go dry, Specter will check fire until all the jumpers are out. At least I'm on the first bird; those ZSU 23-4's shouldn't be tracking on the first bird. If I just get out of the aircraft, I know I'll make it. Hit the ground, link up with anybody from my platoon and bust ass to Dog. I wonder if they're waiting?*

Another message was coming back through the stick; it sounded like the same one from before; "Th.. ..... we're com..." The Ranger next to Hunter turned to him once again, this time a little slower than before, "They know we're coming."

Oh well, these mother fuckers have no idea of the kind of whip ass were going to put down. Hunter turned and relayed the message. *These mother fuckers are going to pay. God, I hope I die with honor,* "This will be the day that I die, this will be the day I die". *Am I going to go to hell for killing another man? God will understand, won't he? I think he will. It's them or me. I hope he'll understand.*

Hunter could see the jumpmaster at the head of the stick again. *Could it be six minutes already?* Another message came back the stick again. "Were going to do the creed." The Ranger creed. Hunter could see the jumpmaster's lips again, and everyone joined in over the ever-present hum of the props:

Recognizing that I volunteered as a Ranger, fully knowing the hazards of my chosen profession, I will always endeavor to uphold the prestige, honor, and high "esprit de corps" of my battalion.

Acknowledging the fact that a Ranger is a more elite soldier who arrives at the cutting edge of battle by land, sea, or air, I accept the fact that as a Ranger my country expects me to move further, faster and fight harder than any other soldier.

Never shall I fail my comrades. I will always keep myself mentally alert, physically strong and morally straight and I will shoulder more than my share of the task whatever it may be. One Hundred-percent and then some.

Gallantly will I show the world that I am a specially selected and well trained soldier. My courtesy to superior officers, neatness of dress and care of equipment shall set the example for others to follow.

Energetically will I meet the enemies of my country. I shall defeat them on the field of battle for I am better trained and will fight with all my might. Surrender in not a Ranger word. I will never leave a fallen comrade to fall into the hands of the enemy and under no circumstances will I ever embarrass my country.

Readily will I display the intestinal fortitude required to fight on to the objective and complete the mission, though I be the lone survivor.

RANGERS LEAD THE WAY!

The adrenaline was now flowing through Hunter's veins as though it had replaced the blood.

"Let's kick some ass," the guy across from Hunter shouted.

"Yeah, let's kick some fucking ass!" He repeated.

Hunter was more than ready to go after sitting without moving for over eight hours. The time was at hand. The time to meet destiny, to serve his country, bring honor to his family, and end the hollow pain that filled his heart. *I know I'll make it if I can just make it to the ground.*

"Six minutes," the command echoed through the aircraft in the voices of all 64 Rangers. *This is it baby, this is it.*

"Inboard personnel stand up," The command was barely audible, but Hunter could read his lips. Hunter had gone through this procedure many times before, twenty-nine times actually, but this time was for real. The jumpers in the center of the aircraft across from Hunter struggled to their feet, pulling each other to the standing position. The process was slow and cumbersome. When all were standing, one crewmember from the aircraft struggled down each side to fold the seats into the up and locked position behind the jumpers. The butterflies in Hunter's stomach grew.

"Outboard personnel, stand up!" the command was echoed through the stick, although it seemed only half the people repeated it. Suddenly everything seemed very hurried. Hunter helped the jumper to his left up, and then started to pull himself up. He couldn't get up. The immense weight on his lap prevented him from rising. As he would begin to rise he would hit the jumpers already standing. A split second of terror flowed through his mind. *I've got to get up quickly. What if the light turns green! I've got to get up NOW!* Two people already standing extended their hands and pulled him up, just as the crewman folded the seat next to Hunter to the upright position. Hunter struggled to bring himself to a fully upright position; the weight of the equipment and the ruck pulled heavily on his lower back. This was always the worse part. Standing with the leg straps of his parachute harness cutting into your groin so the opening shock won't catch your nuts, hunching slightly over as the weight pulls your body forward and your shoulders over. He could feel his heart pounding, the blood racing through his veins, breaths quickening.

"Hook Up," the command was muffled and seemed to blend in with the noise of the aircraft. Hunter knew the command was coming, and knew it was given when he saw people in front of him reaching for their static line. Hunter looked to his chest and fumbled to unhook the locking mechanism from his reserve handle.

Quickly, quickly, I've got to get hooked up! If I don't, I'll be dead. It's a quick 500-foot trip with no chute open. Hunter grasped the hook with his right hand and lifted it toward the steel cable suspended above his right shoulder. The blood seemed to race through his veins so fast that his hand vibrated. It wasn't a shake; it was a vibration. Hunter clipped the hook on the cable and locked it into place. He then struggled to grasp the cotter key suspended from a small string below the hook. When he secured the key, he pushed it through the safety hole on the hook. He pulled hard. *There are no second chances if this hook breaks or doesn't work.* It was tightly secured.

"Check Static Lines," again the sounds were barely audible, but Hunter could see the "OK" sign the jumpmaster gave with his hand. Hunter pulled down hard on the yellow cord again, just to make sure. *This is it, this is it, this is it.* Just then the aircraft pulled up. The unmistakable feel of hundreds of extra pounds pulled on his back emphasizing the movement. Hunter turned and looked out the window on his left side. The pitch-blackness of night was suddenly struck with two very bright flashes, one after the other, so close they almost looked simultaneous. It reminded him of lightning in the dead of night.

Another message was rapidly flowing back the stick, one after the other quickly turning over his shoulder to repeat it. "THE BOMBS ARE IN!" *Yeah, yeah, yeah.* The jubilant anticipation showed on every camouflaged face. Hunter's heart seemed to beat out of his chest. "LET'S GET SOME!" he shouted to the man in front of him.

"I hope God will forgive me for this."

The rest of the jump commands were given very quickly. "Check Equipment.....Sound Off For Equipment Check." The hurried response came through the stick. Each man tapping the one in front of him on the shoulder to indicate they were OK. The safety man seemed to move down the stick at lightning speed, stopping only briefly at each man to ensure they were hooked up and ready.

When the doors were opened, it felt as if the heat from hell had swept through the aircraft. It had been very cold in Benning when Hunter had loaded the aircraft, probably in the low 40's. Now the scorching heat of the jungle invaded the space; he began to sweat instantly. "I wish I had taken off my long john bottoms like they told us to," Hunter thought. He could faintly smell the pungent sweetness of the jungle. "This will be the day that I die, this will be the day that I die. Those good old boys were drinking whiskey and rye, sing' in..."

The plane began to shake violently, back and forth, back and forth. It was difficult to stand as the aircraft undulated and shook. *Just get me out of here! If I make it out of the aircraft, I know I'll make it.* Hunter's only thoughts were to get out of the aircraft. GREEN, GREEN. Hunter could see the red light by the door turn green. We're over the drop zone!

Hunter could see the stick moving. The first people were exiting the aircraft. Out of the corner of his eye he saw the man across from him fall to the floor violently. Holes appeared in the skin of the aircraft just on the other side of his body. *THEY DIDNT GET THE FUCKING ANTI AIRCRAFT GUNS! MOTHER FUCKERS!* The people immediately behind the man were unhooking to move around him, then hooking back up to jump.

Hunter's stick was moving. Three people left, two, one, his thoughts were of getting out of the aircraft FAST. *I'm going to run over this mother fucker in front of me if he's not quick enough.* The plane shifted hard to the left. The man in front of Hunter slammed into the side of the aircraft as he started to move forward. Hunter reached out with his hand to push him down the aisle faster, but he snagged. A piece of his 1950 weapons case was hung up on the corner of one of the folded up seats. He tried to bend down and free himself but the gear he had hanging from his body inhibited the movement. Hunter reached down, and pulled hard on his weapons case, it was still hooked. *I'VE GOT TO GET OUT!!!* An instant of panic began to grip him. Hunter pulled the case again as hard as he could. It came free!

"GO,GO,GO!" Hunter screamed. Both ran for the door, Hunter's hand pushing him by his parachute. The plane shifted violently to the left. Hunter stumbled as he came to with in ten feet of the door. The man in front of him ran through the open door. Hunter looked for the safety man who was suppose to be at the door to hand him his static line as he had done so many times before. He was gone; so was the jumpmaster. "They must have fallen out or got hit," he thought. Hunter threw his static line forward and leaped for the door.

CHAPTER 7

It was a bad exit. Hunter's body form was terrible. The wind struck him with an uneven thrashing, and he immediately began to spin. The ocean of loud noise inside the aircraft became a sudden sea of silence. The opening shock was hard. POW! Hunter struggled to look up at his chute but his risers were twisted behind his head, impeding movement and pushing his helmet forward. There was a soft pop sound, then another. Pop....pop.... pop. Then a loud CRACK. CRACK. CRACK...CRACK..pop.....pop. Hunter looked down. He could see the streaks of green and then red shooting across a large, long strip illuminated by the moonlight. He continued to spin. Then the red streaks that seemed to be going so slow he could catch them, moved just past him toward the sky. At first it didn't even register that these were bullets.

"*Man, that is pretty*," Hunter thought. CRACK...CRACK...CRACK. The tracers moved majestically over his head. Hunter looked up again to see the streaks flow through the fabric of his chute. Hunter grabbed and released the strap to lower his rucksack. WHAM.

Hunter hit the ground hard, falling onto his left side. CRACK,CRACK, CRACK. He had landed in a small indented waterway amidst a slight opening of the jungle canopy. About 100 meters on the south side of the runway. CRACK, CRACK, CRACK. Hunter was getting it from two directions. The rounds were hitting the dirt on the rim of the five-inch deep ditch near his head, kicking dirt in his face. CRACK, CRACK, CRACK. He was on his back. As he looked in the direction of the sounds he could see two of them spread about 25 meters apart, 30 meters from Hunter at the edge of the clearing. CRACK, CRACK, CRACK.

Hunter desperately slithered on his back down the furrow to get away, moving one shoulder after the other as fast as he could. CRACK, CRACK, CRACK. The rounds were now impacting just below his feet. The lowering line that connected Hunter to his ruck pulled tight and began to drag.

CRACK, CRACK, CRACK. *They must have seen the movement of my ruck and directed their fire there.* Hunter fumbled with the clip where his lowering line connected to his D ring. It was stuck. *Holy shit, I'm dead, I'm dead, I'm dead.* It felt like a movie, almost real but not quite. Hunter reached down and found his knife. He released the button on the strap, pulling the 8-inch blade free, grabbed the line with the other hand and cut it.

From the corner of his right eye he could see a dark shadow emerging from the tall elephant grass only ten feet from where he lay. It seemed to fly directly at him like a wreath bent on destruction, the only characteristic that distinguished the shape from a ghost was the clear outline of an assault rifle. The man was charging him like a bull, as the flashes from the assault rifle he brandished denoted the shots. CRACK, CRACK.

CHAPTER 8

Emil had just finished his midnight rounds around his area when the phone rang in the small guard shack.

"Emil, Emil, Emil, THE AMERICANS ARE COMING!!!!" a voice shouted from the phone.

Emil knew the voice; it was the commander of his section – Jose Ortega.

"Jose, calm down," Emil responded in a cool and collected tone. "Tell me what you are talking about."

"I received a call from the head of El Presedente's security detail, the Americans are coming!"

Emil's superiors had briefed them days ago to be on heightened alert because of the possibility that the Americans would try to overthrow Noriega and take over the country. It never really seemed possible though, and if they did – they would be in for a great battle. Now that the news had come, the startling reality of the situation was coming to bear. They would surely come down the road from their base at Howard Air Force Base.

"What are my orders Jose?"

"Deploy your men along the road to ambush them when they come, send two of your men to the anti-aircraft guns in case they try to bomb us. They must not be allowed to capture El Presidente."

Emil stood straighter, "I understand," he said as he hung up the phone.

Emil had been made a squad leader from his induction into the Panamanian Army. Now he would get an opportunity to put to use all he had learned about tactics and leadership in combat. He had lead his men on many raids in the highlands against drug runners, at least the drug runners who did not pay their proper tribute to the government, but nothing against professional soldiers. Emil had often seen these soldiers out in Panama City and wondered how tough they really were, now he was going to find out.

Emil deployed his squad of seven men along the road with anti-tank weapons, putting two more on the anti-aircraft ZSU 23-4s in his area. He didn't think the Americans would bomb the compound and risk killing El Presidente, but you never could tell. The Americans liked to show off their technology.

Just as the thought passed through his mind, another more disturbing one crept in. What if they send in their Special Forces from the sky? Just then there were two massive explosions toward the barracks. It seemed the entire world was transformed into day for a moment as the massive bombs exploded.

Emil looked up just in time to see the first C-130 fly over the runway spewing parachutes from both sides of its body. Then the thunderous roar from the ZSU 23-4s filled the night with the rhythmic sound of machine gun fire and streams of tracer lights streaked into the sky like mini shooting starts.

"THEY ARE COMING FROM THE SKY!!!" Emil screamed. He raised his AK-74 Assault rifle and began shooting skyward. It was only a second and the parachutes already seemed to be hitting the ground. A dark figure flew over his head and into a small clearing in the jungle only 25 meters from his position.

Emil sprayed the area with the remaining rounds in his magazine, inserted a fresh clip and charged the figure in the shadows of the jungle opening.

CHAPTER 9

Without thinking, Hunter rolled over his side toward the invading spirit, springing into a low crouch, knife in hand. He met Emil in mid stride, blocking his rifle to the outside of his body with his left hand. CRACK, the rifle expended another round.

Hunter ducked under Emil's arm and flipped him over his shoulder in a firemen's carry, the knife fell to the ground at Hunter's feet.

Emil immediately sprung to his feet, drawing his own knife. Hunter reached down to retrieve his own blade.

With the speed of a man possessed, Emil slashed his knife back and forth in front of his body as he charged the enemy.

Hunter stepped to the side and avoided the first two blows, but as he moved again he became entangled in his parachute lines. The pull was just enough to throw him off balance and Emil's blade slashed across the top of his hand. Hunter crouched slightly and thrust his own knife into Emil's face.

The blade missed by only millimeters as Emil dodged to the side. After a slight recoil, Hunter thrust the knife forward - again the blade just missing Emil's face but slicing into his ear.

Emil let out a yelp of pain. The heavy blade on the combat knife had cut off the top 1/3 of his ear. It hung in a grotesque fashion by a small piece of cartilage on the very rear. Emil swore as he cupped his hand over the damaged flesh, pulling it away to see the blood.

In the slight pause, Hunter reached up and pulled the quick release on his right shoulder, then his left allowing the parachute to fall away from his body – never taking his eyes off the enemy soldier standing only ten feet in front of him.

In the moonlit opening in the jungle, the two figures stared at each other for several seconds. In the near distance the pops from rifle fire echoed through the trees.

"Come on you American Pig!" Emil spat as he lowered the hand from his bleeding ear.

Hunter reached forward with his left hand and gestured with his fingers, cupping them to the rear. "Come on".

The gesture seemed to fuel his rage, and Emil again charged forward thrusting his blade back and forth in front of his chest.

A burst of automatic fire stitched a path between the two, as they both hit the ground - Emil veering from his path toward Hunter and rolling away. The rounds flew over the top of both men, the tracers streaking just inches above their heads.

Hunter crawled feverishly toward his assailant, pausing only for a second to switch the direction of the knife in his hand. He quickly twirled the blade to a downward position in his fist and continued moving as the bullets cracked over head.

Emil had glanced toward the direction of the fire when he noticed the rapidly approaching Hunter scurrying across the ground. Hunter raised the knife and struck down with the fist. Emil caught the blow mid flight and blocked it with his own knife hand; redirecting it just enough to slide harmlessly off his side. He reached across with his free fist and slammed it into Hunter's face.

The blow only stunned Hunter for a split second, he rolled back off his side and up into a crouch.

Emil too rolled away from his adversary and up to his feet. With a loud scream he charged Hunter with all the strength he had left.

Emil's movement carried him directly through Hunter and his waiting knife. His blade jabbed toward Emil's stomach as Emil jumped to the side, the knife tearing through his clothing and slicing into his side. At the exact same moment the knife ripped through his camouflage top, Emil thrust his own blade toward Hunter's chest. Hunter pushed his adversaries arm away with his free hand as he felt the sharp sting of the metal as the blade sliced across his own ribs.

They were face to face when they came to a halt on the ground. A grotesque exhale of air escaped Emil's mouth as he stared deep into Hunter's eyes. The smell was lurid, it seemed to be a combination of fish, tobacco, and blood. Then, as if sparked by the same bolt of lightening both men pushed away from the other and stood.

CRACK, CRACK, CRACK, CRACK. Another burst of automatic fire sprang from the jungle, just missing both men as they hit the ground ten feet from each other. Emil rolled and sprinted toward the white buildings.

As he watched him leave, Hunter realized that he was still in his parachute harness. He quickly squirmed to get free. CRACK, CRACK,

CRACK. The shots began to come again from the two people in the opening. The rounds hitting close to Hunter's head..

Hunter desperately pawed on the side of his weapons case to open it. The top fell open, and he grabbed the butt of his SAW machine gun. He pulled hard. It came out, but the drum of 5.56 ammunition had come off the gun. The belt of ammo had also pulled out from the feed tray. CRACK, CRACK, CRACK, CRACK, CRACK, CRACK. "Thank God that for this small indent in the jungle floor," Hunter thought, "or I'd be dead already!"

Hunter was still on his back, staying as flat as he could as he frantically opened the feed tray cover of his weapon and shoved the end of the belt in the feed tray. "I'm dead, I'm dead, I'm dead!" he thought.

"COME ON, please feed, Please feed, PLEASE FEED!" Hunter pulled the charging handle back and released it. The round seemed to chamber. He pulled the remainder of the belt free from the green container and rolled around his weapon and onto his stomach, pointing in the direction of the green tracers. CRACK, CRACK.

Hunter could see the dark black silhouette of a man at the originating point of the green tracers. It didn't look like he was wearing a helmet. The tracers seem to emanate from the center of his torso. Behind him there were what seemed to be light-colored buildings. CRACK, CRACK, CRACK; the dirt kicked in Hunter's face again. These rounds were from a figure to the left of the person he now had the cross hairs of his machine gun on. "*Fuck you.*" The weapon rose slightly as he pulled the trigger for a second. Buzzzzzzzit. "*COME ON, MOTHER FUCKERS.*" Buzzzzit. The second burst followed the shape to the ground.

CRACK, CRACK, CRACK, the other one was tracking on Hunter's tracers. The dirt stung his face as it hit his left cheek. Hunter pulled the trigger as he shifted toward the shape that was now dropping to the ground. Buzzzzit. He couldn't see him. The grass between Hunter and the figure was too high. Buzzzzzzzzzzzzzzzzzit. Hunter sprayed the area where he went down. For a split second he scanned the area for movement and began to pull the trigger again, then something fell from the sky on the same spot where the bad guy was. "*FUCK, FUCK, FUCK*". Hunter could hear a variety of different bangs in the distance. His ears were ringing. *No movement, no movement, no movement.* Hunter scanned the area - - nothing. He could see another Ranger just behind the area, falling fast from the sky. Wham, he hit the roof of the building just behind. "That had to fucking hurt," he thought.

I've got to get the fuck out of here. Hunter quickly rolled to his back and finished getting out of his harness, pulling his web belt free. He rolled to his stomach again and began to crawl in the direction of the runway. The buildings were now 50 meters to his right. Hunter continued to slither forward, leaving his ruck behind. *It's just too hot to grab it. I can always come back for it later if I have to. Someone else will have enough C4 to blow the tower.* Hunter soon entered the canopy of the jungle. The familiar sweet stench of the jungle filled his nose.

There was a flashing yellow light that showed like a beacon through the jungle about 100 meters to his left. Hunter couldn't quite make out what it was. *It couldn't be an armored vehicle. Why the hell would that have a yellow strobe light on top?* Hunter instantly thought about the LAW rocket he had left with his ruck, now about twenty meters to his rear. *I could blow that fucker up, whatever it is. No, there's too much vegetation; and I might hit one of my guys.* He couldn't positively ID the target.

BOOOOOM. There was a large explosion in front of the truck. In the flash Hunter could make out distinct human figures floating away from the epicenter of the explosion, arms and legs spread eagle.

"Burrrrrrrrrrrrrrrrrrrrrrrrrrrrrrrrrrrrrrrrrrrp! *What the hell was that?* The sound came from everywhere. Then there was a swish as a few AH6 helicopters flew overhead. Hunter could hear the A-C130 Specter gunship engaging targets. Boooom, pop,pop,pop. It was a combination of small arms and aircraft. There was also the clamoring, rhythmic beat of a 50-caliber machine gun somewhere in the close vicinity. *Intel didn't say anything about a 50.* Burrrrrrrrrrrrrrrrrrrrrrrrrrrrrrrrrrrp! "What was that long burping sound?" he thought.

Through the trees and vegetation he could see the opening of the airfield; there was another small shack to his ten o'clock.

Movement.

There was someone moving from his right to his left toward the shack. Hunter drew his SAW tight into his shoulder, closed his left eye and sighted down the length of the weapon on the figure. He could hear muffled voices; *was it Spanish of English?* The silhouette of the figure became clear against the lightness of the open airfield as his eye focused. His head! He had the distinct rag head on his helmet that all the Rangers wore to distinguish them from the enemy. *It's was one of my guys*, Hunter thought. As the figure moved closer to the house, Hunter could see two others at the side of the structure. The faint whisper of "Bulldog, bulldog," was now clear.

Hunter rose to a crouching position and began to slowly creep toward the building, weaving through the vegetation. As he approached the building, he began to whisper the password, "Bulldog, Bulldog" *"Is it loud enough?"* he thought. Not loud enough and they'll think I'm a bad guy and shoot. Too loud and the bad guys will hear me and shoot. "Bulldog,

Bulldog, Bulldog," a little louder as he approached. The figure at the side of building waved him in. Hunter quickly scrambled to a crouching position at the side of the wall.

"Who is this?" the figure asked. Hunter recognized his platoon sergeant.

"Hunter," he responded.

"Get ready. We've got to get to the other side of the runway," he said.

Looking across and down the length of the runway Hunter could see different color tracers zinging from one place to another. Booooom, a flash lit up the sky as a 105 from Specter hit something on the other side of the runway, about 200 meters away. Hunter could hear some distant screams in Spanish. It sounded like two of those mother fuckers. Booooom, another flash in the same area.

Two other guys came running in, announcing the running password as they scrambled up. As he looked around the area, Hunter could see about twelve Rangers, all fanned out in a hasty perimeter facing out in all directions. Hunter knelt at the edge of the building about ten meters from his platoon sergeant, scanning the area.

"Those little fuckers are everywhere," a guy from his platoon whispered as he entered the perimeter and knelt beside Hunter.

"I know," Hunter replied. "Guess they weren't in the barracks when the bombs hit."

"Did you see that truck with the light on top?" he continued

"Yeah," still whispering "What the fuck was that?"

"A tanker truck. I almost shot it with my LAW till I saw the guy standing beside it with his hands up, scared shitless. He must be a civilian just delivering gas."

"What the hell was that explosion, just in front of that fucker?" Hunter inquired.

"I don't know, when I came through there, there were about four LBG's scattered all over the place with pieces missing" he replied.

LBG's were a name that Rangers used for the Panamanian soldiers; it meant "Little Brown Guy's."

The tracers continued to zip back and forth across the runway. Soon there were about fifteen Rangers in the small perimeter around the building. Hunter saw Brady, Vino, and a couple others from his platoon, and his buddy James from first platoon. Hunter took up a spot in the prone position on the edge of the jungle, overlooking the runway, about ten meters from the side of the building. Each Ranger was about 5 meters apart in a circle around the small house. Hunter surveyed the area, watching the tracers, and the large flashes from the Specter's ten5's. Then he saw the source of the sporadic Burrrrrrrrrrp's. He could see the AH6's flying across the opening, engaging targets with their mini-guns and 2.6 inch rockets. The small dark objects, it looked to be 3 or 4 of them, would come in low over the trees and take shit out. Hunter could see them engaging something at the end of the runway. As the aircraft came in, the streaks of the tracers from the mini-gun seemed to form one continuous beam. For every one tracer you see there are seven rounds you don't. The guy on the other end of that thing had to be shredded.

The platoon sergeant scurried over to the guy next to him to giving some direction, then over to Hunter. "We're going to move out across that airfield in two wedges, about twenty meters apart. You're in the first wedge. Get ready to move!" He moved to the next person in the perimeter.

Soon he had made it all the way around. Hunter looked to the corner of the building and could see him give the "move out" gesture. Hunter rose to one knee, then as the guy to his left stood, he stood and followed. He positioned himself ten meters to the rear and right of the point man. Each man successively followed on both sides forming a large V formation. Hunter kept his head on a swivel, moving it back and forth scanning the area for targets. The second group from the perimeter formed another wedge about 25 to 50 meters behind the last guy in Hunters formation. The first 100 meters were uneventful. Hunter could see shapes moving in many different areas, but none engaged them. Most of the time the rag head of their helmet served well to identify them as Rangers.

The second wedge had moved about 25 meters out of the jungle line when the shit hit the fan. Crack..Crack..Crack! *Some of those fuckers are in a building on our left flank.* The rear wedge hit the ground and returned fire, while Hunter's group continued to move. "Keep going, Keep going!" his platoon sergeant commanded from the center of the wedge, waving his hand in the forward motion. Each time Hunter looked over his left shoulder he could see the small firefight progressing. Hunter's formation was now on, then over, the tarmac of the runway. Hunter felt like a sitting duck in the middle of this open area moving briskly across. As they crossed the far edge of the runway, Hunter looked again to see the second wedge advancing on the building. Alternating fire. Every other man would return fire, while the other alternate man would maneuver forward toward the building. They leap-frogged ahead in bounds.

The Rangers, who were still bounding toward the building were now within 25 meters, laying down a heavy volume of suppressive fire. The PDF inside couldn't even return fire, if they were still alive.

Hunter moved forward, scanning the rapidly approaching edge of the jungle wildly for targets. Then everything slowed to a crawl. It felt to Hunter like slow motion in a movie, although he knew it was actually happening very quickly. As he scanned to his right, an AH-6 helicopter gunship swept over the edge of the jungle canopy. *"OH, FUCK. I HOPE HE SEES OUR GUYS!"* Hunter pivoted around to his left to see the building and the firefight. The AH-6 swept toward the building and our guys. 200 meters, 150 meters, 100 meters, 25 meters. As he approached Hunter could see the tracers from his mini gun before he heard the ominous Burrrrrrrrrrrrrrrrrrrp.

"NO, NO, NO, NO, NOOOOOOOOOOOO." *He was on the guns too soon.*

The stream of tracers started about ten meters before the line of Rangers advancing, and continued through the house. The next AH-6 that followed behind launched a salvo of 2.6-inch rockets into the structure. Then the silence. Then the screams.

A sick feeling permeated throughout Hunter's soul. His heart seemed to sink out of his chest. He knew they were dead, *but who?* Hunter's mind rushed back to consciousness in a burst of senses. Everything was back to real time speed, although the whole thing still seemed like a dream.

"Bulldog, Bulldog," the words came from the blackness of the jungle. It was another group of Rangers in a small perimeter. The lead man repeated the same words as he entered the vegetation. Hunter thought this was a bit ironic. *We have always trained to use the challenge and password in these situations and the running password only when you were being pursued by the enemy and needed to identify quickly. It seemed when it was finally real, no one wanted to waste time and risk not being recognized.*

As he entered the perimeter, Hunter recognized the voice--it was his Lieutenant. The officer immediately directed Hunter to a place in the circle of men with a point of his hand. Hunter knew what to do; he had done it countless times before. He quickly glanced to his left and right, there were two other guys from his squad. *This must be our rally point.* Hunter scanned his sector for targets. The guys who had crossed the runway in his wedge that were not in his platoon, were now quickly skirting the edge of the jungle toward their rally points.

A few seconds later Hunter's team leader quickly moved up and patted him on the shoulder. "Who is this?" he said.

"Hunter," he answered.

"Good, you OK?" he whispered.

"Yeah, but I had to cut my ruck away. The shit was too hot when I landed. I don't have any demo, but I do have my blasting caps," he explained, then continued to scan his sector.

"OK. How's your ammo?"

"About 400 rounds SAW, 6 mag's of 5.56, and four frags."

He quickly moved to the next person in the perimeter, then back to the center to relay the information to the Platoon Sergeant. A few seconds later he returned. "We're moving, find some demo from someone who's got their ruck." He moved to the next guy just as the man on Hunter's right began to stand to move--just like an accordion. First the lead guy would rise up, then the next, the next, and so on. The platoon continued to move along the inside edge of the jungle in a Ranger file. They stopped after traveling about 75 meters. Hunter could see a white structure in a clearing about 50 meters from his position, the faint outline of a tower behind it.

"This is dog!" he thought. Hunter moved over to the man next to him and tapped him on the shoulder. "You got any C4?" he whispered. Hunter immediately recognized Lancaster, a guy from his team.

"Yeah, I've got two sticks," he replied.

"I need it."

He rolled onto his side and opened the flap of his ruck while Hunter covered his sector. Lancaster dug in with his hand and produced one stick, then the other.

"Do you have any det cord, and time fuse?"

Another quick search of his ruck produced a small coil of each. "Thanks," Hunter said as he stuffed the C4 in the side cargo pocket of his pants. Hunter put the time fuse and det cord in the other side, picked up his weapon and moved to the guy behind him.

"You got any demo?"

"Yeah, some," it was one of his good friends from first squad, Smitty.

"I need it to blow that tower."

He rolled over and opened the top flap of his ruck, producing four more sticks of C4.

"Thanks buddy." He just nodded and secured his ruck, scanning his sector. Hunter made his way back to his position.

Hunter's team leader approached him again and patted his shoulder. "First squad is going to take out the building. We are going to be in an over watch position about 25 meters from here." He raised his arm to point in a direction just to the right of the house.

"OK," Hunter replied, "I've got enough demo to blow the tower."

He nodded, and headed back to the Platoon Sergeant.

Soon he returned, giving the hand gesture to follow. Hunter stood, moved over to his other team member, tapped him on the shoulder and repeated the gesture. They moved cautiously through the vegetation to the edge of the clearing where the building was in full view. Hunter didn't see any movement inside. He could hear Henry, his team leader, whisper on the radio, "In position."

First squad emerged from the jungle 25 meters to Hunter's left in a spread out Ranger file, and ran toward the building.

Hunter pulled his SAW hard into his shoulder and looked down the metal sights at the building. As they approached, he moved his aim from window to window to door to window. *No movement.* "I can't fucking tell if there is anyone in the windows," he thought. *I won't know until they fire.* The first man was now approaching the building. Hunter instinctively held his breath and drew aim on the window closest to the edge.

Suddenly, there was a glint in the upper left window. Hunter quickly trained his weapon on the refection. Then another flash. Hunter held his breath, then consciously concentrated on his breathing so he could get a good group of shots off, focusing his view down his gun sights to the window. "I've got a possible target." He whispered to his team leader.

"Where?" Henry asked with anticipation.

"Top left window."

"Are you sure?" Henry starred down his rife into the black hole of the opening.

At the same second, both men saw the object protrude from the window.

The jungle erupted in a hale of gunfire as Hunter and his team leader poured a wall of rounds through the opening.

The shape fell forward, out the open window, landing a few feet from the last man in the formation assaulting the house.

The group began to move very quickly. The first man reached the corner. Then the second, third, fourth, and fifth. They were spread out about five meters apart along the side of the building, all crouching. The first man crept around the corner to the edge of the door, ducking under a front window on the way. The second followed, quickly crossing in front to the other side of the door. The others all crowded close together--their weapons pointing in all directions. The one Ranger on the opposite side of the door stepped out from the building kicking the door open. The first man on the opposite side threw a grenade through the door. The entire squad flattened themselves against the wall. The flash radiated through the downstairs windows, and then the muffled boom sounded. The squad entered through the door immediately. All disappeared through the door in a second. There was sporadic, muffled gunfire, definitely 5.56, ours. Hunter didn't hear any AK.

A few seconds later Hunter could barely hear a transmission from his team leader's radio. He turned to Hunter and said, "It's clear." Hunter continued scanning the area. From the corner of his eye he could see Henry key his radio mike. "Roger, we have the demo. We're ready."

Another surge of adrenaline flowed through Hunter's veins. He knew it was demo time. Hunter was the main demo guy for this mission, and now it was time to blow some shit up! His team leader picked up, whispering "lets go." Hunter stood and followed. They ran across the open area to the side of the building, Hunter squatted at the base of the wall.

His Platoon Sergeant came running up, stopping briefly near Henry, then to Hunter.

"Hunter, you ready?"

"Roger Sergeant," he replied. Hunter reached down and unbuttoned the side pocket where he had the C4, holding his weapon with the opposite hand.

Sergeant Miller radioed to the Lieutenant, "Red six, this is red five, we're ready to cut the tower. Over."

Hunter began to extract the sticks from his pocket and lay them in the cradle of his arm between his elbow and his weapon.

Sergeant Miller grabbed Hunter's shoulder as he listened to the mike of his radio; "wait one, he's calling the company commander." Hunter froze in place, still scanning the jungle around the area.

"Hunter. . .," as he listened "they want to keep the tower now. Put the demo away." He moved away to the corner of the building.

"FUCK, FUCK, FUCK." *I wanted to blow that tower up so bad I could taste it.* "Oh well," He thought.

Sergeant Miller swept by again, whispering as he passed; "we're moving, we're moving, get ready."

Hunter finished returning the demo to his pocket, buttoning it, then continued to scan his sector. A second later Hunter's team leader came. "We're moving to the next objective, we're point. Lets go."

Hunter had made it past the first objective, now if he could only live through the next.

CHAPTER 10

He moved out in the opposite direction from which they had just come. Hunter followed closely, making sure he maintained a ten-meter interval between men. Hunter could see that there was a thin row of vegetation between his unit and another structure. He remembered the NCO academy from the satellite pictures they had studied the past few days. He scanned the area frantically looking for targets. The team stopped at the edge of the vegetation--just ten meters shy of the structure. Henry radioed back. "Red five, this is red three bravo, we are at the structure. Over."

Hunter straining to hear if anything was coming from the structure, but all he could hear was the gunfire and explosions from other battles. The response came back in about a minute. "Red three bravo, this is red five. Red six confirms that Intel says the structure is empty. Bypass quickly, we need to get to the next objective. Over."

Hunter wasn't too sure about this. The lieutenant said that Intel had confirmed the building to be empty and we were supposed to move right in front of it to hurry to the next objective. It seemed a little weird; what if some of those fuckers ran in there when we jumped in? They rarely took stupid chances, but this seemed to be one of them.

Henry stood up and motioned Hunter to move. Hunter then motioned to Lancaster behind him. The team crept to the side of the building. Henry quickly glanced around the corner. He looked back at Hunter and whispered, "Clear." The team moved forward.

The building was built in the shape of a large U. The team was crossing at the open end. There seemed to be some type of courtyard in the center of the U, with several trees scattered throughout it. The inside walls of this single-story structure had windows and several doors around the length of the inside perimeter.

The team made it about ten feet from the edge when all Rangers in the group heard it at the same time. Voice's inside the building, and it wasn't

English. The squad immediately dropped to the ground in a prone position, pointing toward the structure. "Where are you mother fuckers?," Hunter though as he sighted down the barrel of his SAW at the first room. Henry picked up and moved back to the side of the building (the very top of the U) where they had just entered. Hunter covering his movement. *No targets.*

When he was safely at the wall, Hunter picked up and moved. Hunter took a position at the corner, peeking around the edge into the courtyard. *No targets.* Henry radioed back, the anticipation clearly presented it's self in his voice. "RED FIVE, THIS IS RED THREE BRAVO. WE HAVE ENEMY IN THE STRUCTURE! OVER." He leaned down. "Do you see them?"

"Negative," Hunter replied

It was an awkward situation. The open end of the U faced the wide-open area of the runway. A road ran in front of the building about ten meters to the team's rear. There was no cover for an over watch and the people inside the structure had a clear shot of anyone inside the courtyard. It was a bad place to be.

More information through the radio. "Roger that, it sounded like they were in this first room. Over." Henry replied. After a short pause, he answered again. "Roger that." He bent down to Hunter, "We're going to take out that first room."

Hunter could hear his team leader unsnap the strap that held a grenade. "You kick, I'll frag em. You've got low and left, I'm going high and right."

Hunter nodded. Another huge surge filled his body. He rose to a knee, again scanning for targets. Henry tapped his shoulder and Hunter moved around the corner. There was a window between the team and the first door; Hunter crouched low and underneath it, Henry following. Hunter reached the door. It was closed. He slowly grabbed the handle and gently turned it. It was unlocked. Hunter cracked the door a fraction of an inch to ensure it wasn't bolted. He looked over his shoulder into Henry's eyes and nodded, making sure he saw him. He grasped the frag at chest level, pulling the pin. He let the spoon fly to cook off the grenade for two seconds. Hunter turned and stepped out in front of the door and then kicked it in the center with a front kick. The door flew open. Hunter slammed himself against the wall beside the door. Henry reach around and threw the frag through the open door at the ceiling, slamming himself back against the wall beside Hunter.

Hunter held his breath. The seconds before the explosion seemed like hours. Everything seemed to happen in slow motion again. Hunter could hear the people inside scurrying around at a frantic pace.

The blast was deafening. Hunter entered the room first. Crouching low; and moving to the left wall. The entire room seemed to be on fire. Smoke was everywhere. It was some kind of barracks room with bunks on either side. The grenade must have landed on the mattress of one of the top bunks. It was now burning in a wild blaze.

Hunter sprayed the room from the center to the left wall with bullets. The choking smoke coupled with the intense light of the fire made it hard to see. Henry entered directly behind him and sprayed the room from the center to the right. Everything seemed to stop. It seemed to be ghostly silent except for the sound of the fire and the ringing in his ears from the explosion.

"NO MAS, NO MAS!" a voice screamed in Spanish. Then a chorus of voices joined in with the same words. "NO MAS, NO MAS, NO MAS!"

Hunter's eyes caught a movement from where the sounds were coming from. In the corner of the room, with a mattress over them, was a group of three PDF soldiers. He swung his weapon toward the threat, sighting on the center of the group. All three immediately threw their hands in the air. The instant contrast of night and light made it impossible to make out the faces, but the gestures were clear. As the three began to emerge from behind their make-shift cover, others in the room began to do the same. Several different spots suddenly protruded with a mass of humanity. Hunter swung his weapon from left to right in an attempt to cover all of them as they emerged. An instant wave of panic drove into Hunters brain; *I can't cover all of these guys, what if one of them has a weapon?*

"NO MAS!" the group screamed in unison.

Hunter grabbed the closest PDF by the shirt with his left hand and through him out the open door he had just entered in. The small framed man flew through the air as he was lifted from the ground by Hunter's powerful hand. Quickly Hunter repeated the action for the next closest PDF, and the next and next. When the last of this bizarre assembly line passed, it appeared that there were two left on the floor.

Hunter heard the distinct voice of one of his guys outside the room. "FUCK, FUCK. . . GET THE FUCK DOWN, GET THE FUCK DOWN!"

Hunter spun around and leaped for the door to help. As he emerged, he thought he was dead for sure. There were PDF soldiers pouring out of each opening in the structure. PDF were rushing out of all the doors of the building in droves. "Why aren't they firing?" Hunter thought. It seemed to him to be a herd of bodies flying into the courtyard. Hunter thrust his weapon to his shoulder and sighted in the direction of the closest bunch.

"NO MAS, NO MAS," seemed to be coming from everywhere.

"GET THEM DOWN," screamed his Platoon Sergeant. Several Rangers were spread out, throwing PDF to the ground with their non-firing hands. Hunter grabbed the closest one and pulled him down. They all seemed to follow in a giant wave. Falling to the ground one after another. There were so many, the ones still coming through the doors had no place to lie on the ground. They had to walk over a human road of bodies to the middle of the courtyard before finding an open patch of ground. Hunter dropped to one knee at the edge of the wall as they continued to pour out and into the open area.

Finally it seemed they were all out. The entire courtyard, which Hunter guessed to be 50 foot deep and wide, seemed to be full of whimpering PDF.

Henry, who had joined in getting people down, moved to Hunter briskly as he listened to his radio. "We've got far side security, with third squad." He picked up and started moving across the open area between both sides of the U. Hunter followed, motioning for Lancaster and Brady.

On the other side of the structure about 25 meters, third squad was spread out on the top rim of a small valley. The team moved up to their left flank, next to the road. Hunter's team leader placed him in a position so his machine gun could cover down the road. Hunter could see flashes from different areas, and the streaks of tracers from a few mild firefights. Things seemed to be well under control. Along with the sounds of gunfire, he could hear the unmistakable sound of the Specter gun ships circling above. For the first time, Hunter looked skyward and saw the lethargic outline of a C-130 flying around the area. It made him feel safe. He didn't see the AH6's anymore. *They must have been sent to a different objective.* The team remained in this position for about fifteen minutes. Henry went to each member of the squad to get their status.

Just then Hunter noticed a nagging burning on his right side, just under his arm. He unbuttoned his BDU jacket and stuck his hand inside. He could feel a deep gouge cut from his side and the sticky wet moistness that could only be blood. "That fucker must have clipped me with one of those rounds from his AK," He thought. He buttoned his BDU top back up. *The bleeding has stopped, I'll be OK.*

Henry came to his position once again. "Get ready to move, we're going to transport these prisoners down to the collection point." Hunter rose to one knee as he went to each man in the squad and repeated the information. Henry then motioned for the team to follow, and they made their way back to the courtyard.

First squad still had them all face down in the middle of the courtyard. I then saw Sergeant Frost. They were questioning some of them, to sort out the officers I'm sure. Since Sergeant Frost spoke Spanish, he was doing the talking. They took a knee as the first group was told to get up, put their hands on their head, and move to the road, in Spanish by Sergeant Frost.

About fifteen were in a line marching toward us. As they approached, they stood and walked beside them. Hunter was in the middle. Sergeant Singer, from third platoon lead, followed by Henry, Hunter, Lancaster, and Brady.

"Make sure you watch those mother fuckers," Sergeant Miller warned as they departed from the courtyard. Hunter knew what he meant. One of these guys might have concealed a gun or a knife even though he was already searched. Hunter had remembered from his operations order that the prisoner collection point was about 100 meters down the road, toward the ocean. Hunter tentatively rotated his watch from the prisoners to the area around covering the group's movement. Soon he could see movement to our front, and what sounded like a very pissed off guy speaking Spanish. Then "Halt." Hunter's squad was being challenged by the platoon that had secured this area. The response from Sergeant Singer was muffled as his back was toward Hunter. Then the voice from the dark continued, "Advance to be recognized." It was standard procedure to make certain who was coming into their perimeter. Sergeant Singer moved forward and conversed with the Ranger who had challenged him, then gestured to move forward.

As they entered their perimeter, Hunter could see where the Spanish voice was coming from. An interrogator had a PDF on his knees with his hands tied behind his back, sitting upward. The interrogator asked him a question in Spanish, and the PDF shot back with one or two words-- probably obscenities. The interrogator drew back and slapped the guy with an open hand across the face then backhanded him on the return motion. He repeated the question. Hunter kept glancing in that direction to watch as he guarded the prisoners.

The squad turned the prisoners over to people at the collection point and headed back in a Ranger file. The group repeated this sequence several times. On the third trip, things got interesting. The squad was about half way to the collection point when a prisoner made a sudden movement. He took his hands down from his head and reached for his shin with his back toward Hunter. Hunter reacted instantaneously drawing a bead on his mid section while screaming, "FREEZE!" The enemy soldier jerked upright, lunging forward with a knife in hand. A determined look of hatred on his face. Hunter met the advance with a front kick, planting the heel of his jungle boot directly in the man's chest. The pressure from Hunters kick sent the 150-pound man flying to the rear, while the knife fell to the ground. "What the fuck are you doing," Hunter exclaimed, his weapon still trained on the man's chest.

The progression stopped as Lancaster came forward.

"What's going on?" Lancaster asked

"This mother fucker tried to stick me with a knife from his boot," Hunter explained. The look on the man's face was still chiseled in defiance.

"Flex cuff this fucker"

Lancaster produced a plastic wire tie strip from his butt pack.

"On your stomach now!" Hunter commanded

The man didn't move.

Lancaster grabbed him by the collar pulling him forward with a jerk, putting the man's face in the dirt. He grabbed his right hand first, then his left, positioning them in the center of the man's back. Putting the loop of the cuffs over both hands, he pulled them tight, binding the man's hands together.

Hunter knew Lancaster was from somewhere in New England, he had the slight accent to prove it. His boyish face normally had a smile on it, his non-descript features reserved. The thing about Lancaster that always amazed Hunter, and the rest of the squad for that matter, was the fact that he could produce basically anything that was needed, even in the middle of nowhere. If you need a tool, he had it. If you needed something to fix something, he had it. One time on a training mission the squad needed to hot wire a car, Lancaster proudly produced a jumper wire from his ruck sack. If you needed it, the guy had it.

They continued the trip.

The trips went on and on, back and forth, back and forth, until finally they had delivered the last prisoner. The lightening in the sky on the eastern horizon indicated the approach of morning. Hunter's squad took a position around a tree in the middle of the courtyard, guarding the new CP.

CHAPTER 11

As the first direct rays of the sun rose, Hunter could hear the traffic on his Platoon Leader's radio. Different situation reports were being given, then the casualty list. The list began. Hunter subconsciously held his breath. The first couple of Rangers he knew of, but didn't know well. Then it seemed that every sound in the universe went quiet. James Bruno. It was James whom he saw get hit.

It wasn't real, it couldn't be real. This had to be a dream. Hunter knew that there was no way that his friend, who he had just been talking to yesterday afternoon was dead.

Sergeant Frost his squad leader approached on his way back from a meeting at the makeshift company command post in one the rooms of the building they had cleared the night before.

"Alright guys," referring to the squad, "get some sleep. First squad is pulling perimeter security until 16:00 tonight. It looks like we may have a special mission for tonight, everybody needs to be fresh. We can rack out here under this tree. So go ahead and get some chow and relax."

Everyone in the group nodded and began to settle in.

"Oh yeah. Make sure you keep your weapon close; they're expecting a counter attack some time today or tonight. Get some rest."

"Sergeant Frost?" Hunter inquired

"Yeah Hunter." he responded.

"I had to leave my ruck in the jungle last night where I landed, the shit was too hot to bring it with me."

"Do you know where it is?" Sergeant Frost asked.

"Roger Sergeant. I can find it."

"Alright, Henry." Sergeant Frost announced in Henry's direction.

Henry jumped up from his position under the tree ten meters away and moved smartly to where the two were standing.

"Yes Sergeant?" Henry asked.

"I need you to go with Hunter to get his ruck."

"Roger Sergeant." Henry responded.

Henry was the typical build for a Ranger, not very large – in fact very skinny. Hunter worked out constantly so he had a muscular build, Henry was the exact opposite. His scant 150 pound frame was built for distance. Most Rangers could run like the wind, Henry was the epitome of a distance runner. His face was very expressive, if he was mad it came across loud and clear. Hunter had seen him put many different Privates through the ringer in his time in Battalion.

As they walked Hunter reflected on his trek through the Ranger Battalion and his life. Hunter always had a positive attitude in everything he did, as far as everyone knew. This attitude served him well in the military. In Basic Training he volunteered for anything and everything. If the Drill Sergeant needed people to do extra work, he would raise his hand. If they needed people to pull extra guard duty, he raised his hand. It was actually a very strategic, and somewhat selfish, move on Hunter's part. In talking to a friend he had met long ago about the Army, Hunter had asked for advice. The advice he was given was to volunteer for everything at first, then when they get to the real shitty jobs and you volunteer they won't make you do it because you volunteered for everything else. This philosophy worked like a charm. Hunter would volunteer, do the best he could at what ever the task was, and when it came time to clean the latrines or another very undesirable job – he was off the hook.

Hunter and Henry started out across the runway that was such a hazard in the middle of the night. Past the shack where he had made his link up, Hunter leading the way.

When they started to enter the jungle, both men instinctively went into a combat patrol mode. Who knew if there were still a few of them hiding in here somewhere. The area had been secured, but there were still plenty of places that the bad guys could be hiding.

As they crept into the jungle the opening that Hunter had fell into the night before became clear. There among a backdrop of elephant grass was a body, still lying on its side. At first glance, he appeared to be guarding a rucksack, Hunter's rucksack. Hunter cautiously approached, scanning the entire area for any hostiles.

His eyes were still open, Hunter noticed first. He was wearing an old pair on camouflage BDU's dirty from what looked like weeks of grime. The front of which had discolored a very dark, almost black, shade of red. He wasn't wearing any boots, both feet were bare. The flies had already started to gather in the scorching heat of the jungle, as the smell of death filled the air.

"Is that one of yours?" Henry whispered.

"The fucker almost got me," was all Hunter needed to say.

Hunter kneeled beside his ruck, trying not to look the man in the face again. He pulled his rucksack over his shoulder, glancing down to see more flies leaving the dead man's partially open mouth.

"Look at your fucking chute man," Henry said while pointing up at the fabric that had floated Hunter to earth last night.

There were several rows of holes extending in various patterns throughout the tapestry.

"Sergeant Henry?" Hunter inquired.

"Yeah."

"Can we take this way back?", motioning toward the group of white building on the edge of the clearing.

"Go ahead. Let's just not fuck around; I want to get some sleep before we head out on our next mission."

The two made their way to the structures.

As they emerged from the vegetation of the jungle, Hunter could smell it way before he could see it. Death. One body was laying face down, a large piece of his head missing. The blood had pooled on the ground under the man's head, insects everywhere devouring their new feast. The smell was nauseating and made Hunter gag.

"Look at that poor bastard," Henry remarked.

Hunter turned to his right to see another dead enemy soldier. The man was lying on his back, red patches every couple of inches extended from his mid section through his head. One of his eyes appeared to be missing; the blood from this soldier's moment of destiny was splattered against the white wall of one of the structures.

"Let's get out of here," Hunter replied.

Both men made their way back to the tree in the middle of the courtyard.

Hunter still couldn't believe that James was gone, there just wasn't any way. He had everything to live for. Hunter hadn't known a better person, always happy, always motivated, always there to help anyone out if they needed it. There must be some kind of mistake.

Maybe if he slept, he would wake up and James would be back. Hunter opened the flap of his ruck, ate his MRE and closed his eyes.

CHAPTER 12

Emil ran, ran as fast as he could. They seemed to be everywhere. They kept coming from the sky, more and more of them. There was only one thing to do, run. His ear stung, but it would not stop him from his revenge, the pigs would pay.

"I will find my compadres in the jungle and then we will attack!" he thought, as he blindly crashed down a path he knew well. He had walked the path many times on his patrols but now running down the darkened corridor he smashed into the trees on one side then the other. He stopped for a second to catch his breath. He could hear the sounds of helicopters and explosions coming from the compound. *I must find the mortar position that is along this path*, he thought. Emil squinted his eyes to try to peer down the path, but the triple canopy jungle made it impossible to see more that just a few feet. He could feel the blood pouring down his neck so he took out a piece of cloth that he used to dry sweat from his face and pushed it hard against his mutilated ear.

"I must stop this bleeding," Emil muttered under his breath as he continued to walk down the path.

I must be getting close, he thought as he walked slowly down the path. I do not want to be shot by my own compadres, I must let them know that it is me.

"Fernando" Emil cautiously whispered. There was no answer. In the distance there were more explosions. He walked a few steps more. The sounds of gunfire echoed through the vegetation.

"Fernando" he once again whispered, a little louder this time. Still nothing. He walked a few more paces.

"ALTO" a voice rang out in the night. Emil froze in place.

"Fernando, it is me – Emil!"

"EMIL, WHAT THE FUCK IS GOING ON?" the frightened voice exclaimed.

"We are being attacked, hurry and help me into your bunker. I need some medical attention.

A figure appeared from the darkness and grabbed Emil's arm.

"WHO IS ATTACKING US MY FRIEND?" Fernando screeched.

"It is the American pigs; they have come for El Presidente. Hurry and get me some gauze and tape."

Fernando led Emil into a small bunker a few feet off the path. Inside, the light revealed a small sandbagged room with a tin roof. There was a TV on in the corner, but all that showed on the screen was torrent of static.

Fernando ran to a box next to the television and retrieved a roll of gauze, a pair of scissors, and a roll of medical tape. He scurried back to Emil.

"Here, sit under the light my friend." Fernando grabbed a folding metal chair from the edge of the room and placed it in the center under the light.

Emil sat on the chair and removed the makeshift bandage he had been using to stop the blood.

"Fuck, my friend – the top part of your ear is missing!" Fernando retorted in disbelief.

"YES I KNOW, JUST BANDAGE IT FOR ME!"

"Bandages will not be enough, I must stop the bleeding."

"How are you going to stop the bleeding? We must hurry."

"I will cauterize the wound with my lighter. It will hurt, but it will stop the bleeding." Fernando reached into his pocket and pulled out his lighter. "I learned this in the School of the Americas".

"Just hurry, we must find a way to counterattack".

Fernando tilted what was left of Emil's ear up toward the light. He then struck the lighter and a flame appeared.

Emil could see the flame from the corner of his eye, he closed both eyes tightly and braced for the pain.

Fernando pushed Emil's ear together with the thumb and index finger on his opposite hand and put the edge of the flame under the mutilated flesh that was now jetting skyward. The flesh sizzled under the heat and began to turn black. Soon the entire top edge of where the ear used to be was blackened and the blood was stopped.

Emil, who was expecting even more intense pain, was surprised to find that the procedure hurt less than he thought. In fact, it seemed to reduce the throbbing. Emil reached up to feel the afflicted area when Fernando grabbed his hand.

The entire bunker shook as an explosion rocked the area.

"Do not touch it yet, I must put some antibiotic on it." Fernando walked to the box by the television again and retrieved a small tube of antibiotic cream. When he returned he squirted the congealed material all over the top portion of Emil's ear. He then wadded up a bunch of gauze and placed it directly on the wound. He finished the field dressing by wrapping gauze around Emil's head to keep the bandages in place.

"Emil, what should we do now?"

Emil pressed his hand to his ear. "We give those American pigs something to think about. Do you have the 60 millimeter mortar ready to fire?"

"Yes. It is covering our drug lab to the North."

"Let's turn it around to fire on the compound."

"What if we hit our brothers?"

Emil grabbed Fernando by the shirt and pulled his face close to his. "Fuck our compadres, these bastards must pay for attacking us."

Fernando's eyes grew large with fear, "Yes, yes, amigo . . . we must make them pay."

"Good, let's set up that mortar to fire."

Emil and Fernando exited the bunker into the bright sunlight.

CHAPTER 13

BOOM. There was a loud whish, then another BOOM. Hunter immediately jumped to his feet. BOOM.

"GET DOWN!" Some one screamed.

Hunter dove to the ground.

"MORTERS! THERE HITTING US WITH MORTARS!" Someone screamed again. Hunter looked around. He was awakened so suddenly, he had to adjust to his surroundings and remember where he was. It was Sergeant Miller screaming.

There were several moment's of silence.

"FUCK. I'M HIT. I'M HIT!', the shriek came from Sterling laying on the other side of the tree from Hunter, about 5 feet from his position. Hunter could see him grasping his leg in a fetal position, blood pouring out profusely through his fingers.

A mealy of small arms fire filled the air. Hunter could hear stray rounds chipping off of the roof tiles of the structures around him. He rushed over to Sterling.

Hunter reached his position. "MEDIC!" he screamed. "Sterling, just relax man. Your gonna be OK! MEDIC!"

"Fuck it hurts, it fucking hurts, IT FUCKING HURTS!" he exclaimed through short gasps of breath.

A piece of shrapnel had sliced a deep gash across his thigh. As Sterling lifted his hand Hunter could see that the cut was deep, real deep. Blood squirted from a cut artery, rising like a little geyser with each beat of Sterling's heart.

"Where's your pressure dressing?" Hunter asked. "MEDIC!"

"Back on my LBE." Sterling replied while pointing over his shoulder, the color already leaving his sullen face.

Hunter knew he didn't have time to go get it. He gripped the artery with his index and forefinger, pinching hard to stop the flow of blood.

The structure slipped from his fingers as the next blast of pressure from Sterling's heart tried to push its way through. He grabbed it again. Hunter pulled some of the fabric from Sterling's loose fitting camouflage trousers up from below the wound with his opposite hand, covering the gash, and pressed down hard. Sandwiching his hand in the open wound.

Henry came surging up, radio in hand. "Doc's on his way, hang in their Sterling."

The small arms fire seemed to diminish, then stop.

"Are we getting hit?" Hunter asked. Sterling's bottom lip was now quivering as he tried to control the pain.

"No, we're just taking pot shots from the tree line, and they hit us with those mortars. First squad said they got a couple on the radio. They've got Specter taking the rest of them out."

"Fuck it hurts," Sterling's control was awesome, but it was a tough fight. That was one thing about Rangers, no matter how bad it was or how bad it hurt, they always had to act hard-core. It was never taught per se, but it just seemed to be a tradition.

Hunter could see the "Doc" come running around the corner of the building, his medical kit in one hand, his CAR-15 rifle in the other. He came to a sliding halt just on the other side of Sterling.

"How you doing Sterling" he asked.

"Not good Doc." Sterling replied.

"You gotta be doing pretty well, you're not dead. Let me see what we got." Doc nodded toward Hunter.

Hunter released the pressure of his make shift bandage. "Doc, I've got an artery pinched off here."

Doc looked into the opening. "Henry, get me a Med Evac in here. Sterling, it's not that bad. You're gonna be fine." Everyone knew that reassurance was always the first step in treating a wound, and Doc was good at it."

Henry immediately grabbed the mic of his radio and made the call for the med evac helicopter.

By this time, the whole squad had formed a circle around Sterling. Sergeant Frost came running up. "Spread the fuck out, you guys know better than this. One more mortar round like that and it could take out the whole squad." Everyone except for Hunter, Doc, and Sergeant Frost fanned out around the courtyard.

"Sergeant Frost, get in my bag there and grab me a hemostat." Doc stated flatly.

Sergeant Frost stumbled through the array of medical gear in Doc's bag and produced a hemostat. He handed it to Doc.

"Damn Doc, that fuckin' hurts!" Sterling was doing his best to stay in control.

Doc placed the hemostat between his teeth and reached into Sterling's front BDU pocket. "You got your morphine in here like your suppose to?"

"Yeah Doc, Yeah." Sterling replied.

Doc produced an auto injector of morphine. He popped the protective top off, patted a small spot on Sterling's good leg to make sure there was nothing to obstruct the needle, and injected it. He then maneuvered the needle-nose pliers looking hemostat behind Hunter's fingers, pinching them together and locking them into place, securing the artery.

"Hunter, you can let go." he calmly asserted. "Why don't you pop him with an IV while I fix this up. There's a couple in my bag."

Doc grabbed a large piece of gauze from his bag, after opening the protective plastic, and placed it on the wound.

Hunter extracted the bag of IV fluids, a needle with a catheter on it, an alcohol wipe and the small clear hose from Doc's bag. He tore open the wipe and scrubbed down the inside of Sterling's left arm. Sergeant Frost came over on Hunter's side.

"I'll hold that," Sergeant Frost stated.

Hunter handed him the bag of lactated ringers after he had inserted one end of the plastic hose in it, shutting off the valve in the line so the fluid wouldn't leak out. Sergeant Frost held the bag up over Sterling's shoulder as he spoke to him to keep him calmed.

I've done this stuff a ton of times, Hunter thought, *please let me hit the vein the first time.* He took the protective plastic off the needle and pulled the skin on Sterling's inner elbow taut to see the veins. He positioned the needle over what appeared to be the largest one, and stuck the point through the skin. Hunter could feel the pop as it entered the vein, a little blood "flashed" back the needle indicating that he was in. He carefully advanced the catheter into the structure and withdrew the needle, leaving his thumb to pinch off the opening until he had the tube hooked up. He hooked the tube up and released the flow of fluids.

Doc had a pressure dressing done, just as Hunter finished.

"Who's got the pole-less litter?" Sergeant Frost asked to the open courtyard of men. In the distance the familiar sound of a Blackhawk helicopter was approaching.

"I do Sergeant!" Lancaster answered from a position at the outside corner of the structure.

"Get it over here. Hunter go take his position."

"Hang in there buddy." Hunter reassured as he picked up his SAW and ran toward Lancaster's position. It was amazing how fast that morphine worked. Sterling was already calming right down.

Lancaster brought the litter over, and all three rolled Sterling on the nylon structure.

Hunter could hear faint radio traffic from Sergeant Frost's radio, and as he glanced back from his position he could see him pop a red smoke and throw it just in front of the open side of the courtyard. The Blackhawk came in low, flared hard, and landed just feet from the billowing red smoke canister. Two individuals jumped from the aircraft and ran to Sterling's position. After a short discussion, all four carried the patient to the helicopter, Sergeant Frost still holding the IV bag in the air. After he was loaded in, the Blackhawk majestically rose skyward, pointed its nose forward and down, and darted out of sight.

The rest of the day was uneventful, until the squad received their operations order. Ambush.

CHAPTER 14

Emil and Fernando had hastily set up the mortar so that it was pointing toward the compound.

As Fernando lined up the mortar from behind the tube, Emil dropped the 60mm projectile down the cylinder. With a ground thumping thud, the projectile sprang from the tube toward its destination a mile away. Emil took the second shell he was holding in his left hand and repeated the motion. "THUD." The ground shook as the second projective streaked away. He picked up a third that was lying on the ground and repeated the motion. "THUD".

Fernando was adjusting the elevation of the tube for a fourth shot as Emil went inside the bunker to retrieve the next shell. Just as Emil entered the bunker there was a massive explosion that threw him to the ground and the weight of the sandbagged ceiling collapsed on top of him, knocking him unconscious.

The Specter AC-130 gunship circling above scanned the area for any other combatants. The communications officer aboard the lumbering giant called the task force commander on the ground, "Roger Gold One, this is Ghost Rider One Nine. We have neutralized the mortar position on the east side of your objective."

The crew on the AC-130 reloaded the 105mm cannon.

CHAPTER 15

As dusk drew near, the squad prepared. The operations order was usually the start of the prep, although sometimes there would be a much shorter warning order to get things moving. The operations order outlined all the details of the mission, routes, weapons, contingencies, and special concerns.

Sergeant Frost returned and shuffled his notes in preparation for the order administering a string of tasks as he worked. "Henry, make sure everyone has full ammo and frags. Lancaster, fill everyone's water. Brady, check all the night vision. Hunter, get com checks will all the radios and check the batteries."

Hunter stood from his position, and moved toward the PRC 77 leaning against the tree in the middle of the perimeter. As he reached the radio, he stuck his hand out to grasp the handle on the right side of the square box when he noticed it. The blood, Sterling's blood. It had dried in a crust on his hands, fusing with the dirt and camouflage paint that covered his hands. It seemed to cake in the crevices around his finger nails. The ends of his jacket must have been soaking up the fluid as well, the dark stains flowing up the sleeves in obtuse patterns for several inches. *Was it Sterling's blood, or that bastard in the jungle, or was it his own* – he wondered. He continued the movement, pulling the harness over his shoulder in one fluid motion. Radio on one side, weapon in the opposite hand and walked back to his position.

Hunter dropped the radio with his gear and moved out to retrieve the other two small radios in the squad. As he walked to Henry's position, he could see him kneeling over his equipment, inventorying his ammo. Emerging from the opposite side of the building, just on the other side of Henry, was Chambers, Baker, and Remington. These three were part of an M-60 Machine Gun crew, and from the look of their direction of travel, would be along for the ride tonight.

"How's your ammo?" Henry asked.

"I need two drums of 5.56," Hunter responded.

"What about frags?" Henry continued.

"I'm good. What's the word on tonight?" Hunter probed inquisitively.

Henry looked up with a slight grin, "looks like we're going hunting."

"Hooah. Sounds good, I'm ready to administer some justice," Hunter added.

The M-60 crew entered the perimeter ten feet from where Henry and Hunter were kneeling. Chambers, holding the gun across his body, nodded as he entered. Both men nodded back in recognition.

"I need your radio Sergeant," Hunter stated.

Henry reached in the pouch the held the radio on his LBE, unsnapped the button on the flap that held it in, and extracted the radio. "I've got extra batteries in the top flap of my ruck there" nodding at his rucksack, just to his front.

Hunter grabbed the ruck and removed two small batteries. "Do you have any PRC 77 batteries?" he asked as he rapidly scanned the area.

Henry just moved his head back and forth, indicating that he did not.

Hunter grabbed the small communication device, and headed across the perimeter to Sergeant Singers location facing the airstrip.

"Sergeant, I need your 126," Hunter said in a low tone as he approached the Alpha team leader.

Singer, who was in the prone position covering his sector, rolled onto his side and pulled the radio from his utility belt just as Henry had. As he turned, Hunter noticed that he had only a light sheen of camo left on his face, looking more like a coat of dirt that anything. On his left cheek was a crimson smear of red, then droplets speckled his face in a tight diagonal line across his nose onto his forehead and K-pot. His eyes were tired and overcast. He handed the radio to Hunter.

"Any PRC 77 batteries Sergeant?" Hunter asked.

Without making a sound, Singer rolled over to his ruck and unbuttoned one of the outside pockets to produce a battery.

"Hooah Sergeant," was the only response that was needed.

Hunter moved swiftly back to his spot, noting from the suns position that there were only a few hours of daylight left. Lancaster, who had been waiting for Hunter to return, stood and moved to make his rounds around all the members of the squad.

Hunter scanned his sector, then began replacing the batteries in all the radios. When he finished, he checked all the knobs, dials, and antennas. He closed the plastic that they were wrapped in to make them as waterproof as possible, and keyed each mic, listening for the static break on the other two radios. They all worked, making a slight squeal as they were keyed. This usually happened when radios were too close when activated. He would do a regular radio check when each was returned.

Henry looked around to see Chambers and his two assistant gunners staked out by the tree, just on the opposite side of Sergeant Frost. Sergeant Frost stood and motioned Hunter toward him with the wave of his hand. Hunter popped to his feet and shuffled to his squad leader.

"Go around the perimeter and tell everyone that we'll get our op order inside this first room," gesturing to the end room of structure. "Tell them to be there in fifteen mikes (minutes). Don't worry about security, we're inside the battalion perimeter."

Hunter rapidly moved off, stopping at each person in the large circle to transfer the message, dropping off the radios. Ending back in his original position.

The fifteen minutes went by quickly. Lancaster brought by a five gallon water jug he had retrieved from the company HQ, and Brady made his pass to check the night vision goggles. As the interval expired, Sergeant Frost stood and moved to the room he had designated earlier. The M-60 Machine Gun team followed ten meters behind.

Singer stood, gestured to his men in A team, and followed ten meters behind the M-60 Machine Gun team. Each squad moving in a large wedge with a wide dispersion between individuals. As A team cleared, Sergeant Henry stood and followed the same procedure. When each person reached the building, they moved into a line to file through the door.

When Hunter entered the room, he could see that Sergeant Frost had constructed a small makeshift table out of footlockers that had been in the room. A map of the area was spread out over the table. Around the area, single bunks were pulled in a tight semicircle for chairs. The file of Rangers moved into the room and filled in around table, in an almost rehearsed orderly manner.

"Take a seat," Sergeant Frost said in a monotone voice, still pouring over his notes.

Sergeant Frost was a tall man by Ranger standards, about six feet two inches. He didn't have the skinny physic that most people in the Special Operations community had; instead he was of average build. His face seemed to be permanently creased with lines and signs of exposure from hundreds of missions. As he had recounted to Hunter several times, he had spent the four years prior to joining the Rangers in a US Army Unit in Panama. That's where he learned his broken Spanish.

As the last person entered the door and sat down, he started.

"This is the operations order for Alpha Company, 2nd Platoon, 3rd Squad, 3rd Ranger Battalion, which will conduct an ambush on 21, 22 December, in the vicinity of Golf Hotel 09084515."

Operations orders were always very detailed. They would cover everything that was to happen on the mission, and let everyone know where they should be at all times. It gave all the map coordinates, what the squad was looking for, why they were doing the mission, and all the mission parameters. It always made Hunter feel good about what he was going to do. There was no uncertainty. When it was done, he would know everything he needed to know to complete the mission, even if he was the only person left alive. One of the things that Sergeant Frost always emphasized was the fact that no matter what happened, everyone was coming home. Rangers never leave anyone, dead or alive. Hunter remembered how comforting that was when he received his first real combat op order for last night's jump. It was kind of funny now that he thought about it, just a few days ago he was dry and clean bullshitting with his buddies about what they would do on their Christmas leave. Now he was drenched with sweat, covered in dried blood, with the stench of death lingering around him. Some of his buddies would never see their leave or Christmas. *Why would God let them die and not take me?* He wondered.

Sergeant Frost continued with his op order. They would only be moving about a click and a half on the other side of the perimeter. There they would set up an ambush on a major trail that the enemy would probably use in a counter attack. There was also the possibility of a follow on mission, if we located a known encampment in the area, we would raid it. Apparently there was a camp set up around a drug lab somewhere in the vicinity, hidden in the jungle.

As Sergeant Frost finished, he asked for any questions. There were none. "OK, be ready to move out in 45 mikes."

In the 45 minutes, Hunter checked and checked his gear again. He made sure his weapon was clean, his canteens were topped off, and nothing from his equipment would make a sound as he jumped up and down to test. He checked his grenade pins, the pins always made him nervous. If the pins were facing out, they could get snagged on a branch and pulled. In the dark you would never know, until it was too late. "They're all good," he thought.

Crossing friendly lines into "the bush," was always a very structured process. Structured for several reasons, most of which was to ensure that the friendly troops weren't mistaken for enemy. Both exiting and returning. The group leader, in this case Sergeant Frost would make contact with the leader of the area in which the crossing would occur.

They would coordinate the time of departure, expected time of re-entry, radio frequencies, passwords, long and short recognition signals, and the procedures and actions to be taken if the enemy hit while crossing the line. This coordination would be very quick because we were crossing through our own company. It tended to be much more in-depth when you were crossing through someone's area that you were not familiar with.

As Hunter sat waiting for the squad leader to return, he reviewed the operations order. He always did this before a mission. It came from the training he thought. He would be grilled over and over again about an operations order when they were training. A Ranger always has to know everything about the mission, so he can complete it even if he is the only person who is alive. That was one of the key elements that was constantly reinforced in the training.

Sergeant Frost returned, walking briskly, the last remnants of the sunset's lights diminishing behind him. He motioned toward Sergeant Henry with his hand, much like a karate chop, then toward the line where we would cross into the jungle. Everyone knew what this meant. Time to move.

A few butterflies flew through Hunters stomach. It always seemed to happen. It really wasn't fear, he wasn't scared – well maybe just a tad. But more anticipation. It reminded him of the feeling that you get as you move up the big hill of a rollercoaster, but stronger. It's that adrenalin of anticipation, he guessed.

Sergeant Henry stood and began to move forward, Hunter emulating his team leader's movements. The entire squad rose in succession and began to fall into a single column, the 60 team falling in behind Sergeant Frost. The line of soldiers approached the defensive line at the edge of compound. When Sergeant Henry reached the location they were exiting, he knelt where two Rangers were behind a small uprising in the ground. Hunter could see him talking to them, then he could see the person he was talking to key his radio. A few seconds later Henry stood, and moved his arm forward, almost in a swimming motion, indicating that it was OK to move out.

Hunter's heart began to race again. This was always one of the most dangerous times in this type of mission. If the enemy were close, we would be sitting ducks. Slow moving targets in a wide open area. Although the sunlight was almost completely gone, and heavy clouds were spotting the sky, it was still easy to make out silhouettes within 150 to 200 meters.

The movement through the lines was very deliberate. Not too fast, but not too slow either. Just a brisk flow through the killing zone, a zone that the company has set up to guard against counter attack.

The string of warriors walked through the opening and into the dense underbrush of the jungles edge. The remaining light that had made things distinguishable in the open was suddenly gone in the triple canopy of the jungle. At first appearances, the jungle seemed to swallow his team leader as he entered. A giant dark green beast that swallowed people whole. A shiver ran down Hunters back, even though he was covered in sweat in the 90 degree heat.

Hunter reached the jungle's edge a few seconds after Henry, and stepped into darkness. The sounds that were only muffled from the distance of the perimeter were now vivid and crisp, a cacophony of birds, bugs and monkeys. The jungle had its own symphony. A symphony that was both beautiful and sometimes frightening. On Hunter's first experience in this lush green land, during a month long jungle school, he had learned about this living biosphere. He had learned how to live in it, eat from it, and fight in it. The sounds were hard to get used to at first. On his first night during training in the jungle, several people had told him to be very careful at night. Everyone seemed to be genuinely concerned. When Hunter had asked why, the response was; "because the howler monkeys will swoop down in the darkness, drag you into the jungle and beat the shit out of you." It seemed at least semi-logical; the noise the beast made would seem to make it at least the size of a gorilla. It was a gag that the old timers would play on the new guys. They would get the young guys all worked up, so they couldn't sleep with the loud "screams" from the howler monkeys flowing through night. Then in the morning, as the exhausted newbie would be humping through the woods, someone would point out the dreaded howler monkey. A very small, cute little creature with unimposing features. When they pointed this out to Hunter, it seemed as though the monkey was even laughing as guys in his squad chuckled.

In the darkness, Hunter could see the green glow from Henry's night vision goggles. He was checking out the area. As he entered, his eyes began to make the adjustment to the darkness. Hunter stayed close, looking behind him every few steps to make sure that Lancaster, the next man in line, was behind him. They soon were on a trail cut through the jungle by many of the animals. About 50 meters in, Henry stopped and made the gesture for halt. Hunter turned and relayed the message to Lancaster. It was so dark he had to practically get into his face to transfer his message.

When on patrol, stopping always meant moving off the path and forming a small cigar shaped perimeter. If it was going to be a short stop, the squad would just take a knee. If it was going to be more than a couple of minutes, they would move to the prone. Hunter stepped off the trail on the opposite side of Henry. He knew this stop was coming. They always did this when entering a new area, it was the SLLS (Sells) stop that was briefed in the operations order. SLLS stood for Stop, Look, Listen, and Smell. It basically was done to let one acclimate to the new environment.

The sweet stench of the jungle filled Hunter's nose. There was just a hint of death in the breeze as well, but it didn't seem to be close. "Maybe some of the bodies that were hit from our counter fire when they hit us with their mortars this afternoon," he thought. As the minutes drew on, shapes in the jungle began to crisp. Blobs of darkness became the leaves of plants and trees. Hunter switched on his night vision goggles and scanned the area. In the triple canopy of the jungle, they didn't work perfectly, but they did work. The goggles relied on a system that amplified light, if there was really no light at all, they would not work. In the eerie green, he could discern his entire squad spread out along the trail. In the rear he could see Brady; his movements always gave him away, looking at him with his own goggles. Brady raised a hand with his thumb raised. Hunter could almost see the smile that he knew Brady had on his face. Hunter returned the gesture and snapped the device on the head harness he was wearing to keep them in place over his eyes. The head harness was a major pain in the ass. It was hard to keep in place, and often slid with the weight of the goggles. Most people would prefer to let the device hang around their neck, and use them with their opposite weapon hand when moving. Hunter usually did the same, but in the jungle, in combat, he didn't want to risk missing anything. So he would deal with the head harness, winching it as tight as it would go. He knew that they would only have to move about a click to the ambush site, so he wouldn't be fighting them that long.

Henry stood, motioned to move out, and started down the path. Hunter did the same. The path drew gradually up, along an incline that was a small ridge that Hunter had seen on the map. In the distance, over the loud overture from the animals and bugs, a soft rhythmic sound was approaching. It sounded as if someone had a microphone next to a grill where they were cooking steaks, with the volume being turned up rapidly. It was the rain. As the drops fell on the trees above, it seemed to dampen the songs of the beast.

As Henry passed a large rubber tree, he made a sign by swinging his hand above his head, in a lassoing motion, and pointed at the tree. This was the signal for rally point. If for some reason the squad was hit and separated during the movement, the rally points that were designated along the way would be used to link up. When Hunter reached the same point, he looked to the rear to ensure Lancaster was watching, and gave the same signal.

After a half an hour of trudging through the jungle, Hunter had reached his pace count, indicating that they had went the distance that had been drawn in the battle plan for the release point. Hunter stepped forward and grabbed Henry's shoulder, "We're at the RP." Henry motioned for a cigar shaped perimeter. Everyone stepped off the trail on either side as they had done earlier.

"Sent it back, RP" he whispered to Hunter.

Hunter walked back and whispered the same to Lancaster; Lancaster did the same the entire way back through the squad. There was always very little verbal communication when they were on patrol. Obviously you wouldn't want to make noise if you didn't have to or the enemy would know where you are. So the intense training had instilled a set of hand movements and gestures that let everyone know what was going on. Coupled with the operations order, all in the squad knew where they were, what was going on, and how far from the objective they were. Hunter knew that they were only about 25 meters from the large path where they would set up their ambush.

Sergeant Frost came up the trail a few seconds later, followed closely by the M-60 crew and Sergeant Singer. When he reached Henry's position, they all knelt in a tight circle. Hunter could only hear bits and pieces of muffled whispers. He continued to scan the jungle for anything out of place.

The entire circle stood and began to move forward. Henry returned to Hunter. "We're going on the leaders recon and set the 60 in place. We'll be back in 25 mikes. Use radio for far recognition" he said as he handed his 126 to Hunter. "Near is snow – counter farm, near is one red flash. Do you have your red lens?"

"Roger Sergeant," Hunter responded.

"Your in charge here. If we don't come back in 2 hours, call Black 1 (company commander), for backup to come find us. If we're hit, we'll fight our way to you. If your hit, go to the last rally point and we will meet you there, hooah?"

Hunter responded again with another "hooah."

Whenever the squad separated, there was the list of contingencies that was always given. That way, no matter what happened, everyone would know what to do. It was the 5 W's. Who, What, Where, When, and Why.

Henry moved forward to rejoin the group as they disappeared into the night. Hunter moved back to Lancaster. He repeated the same information that was just given to him. When he finished, he moved back to his position as Lancaster passed the info back to the person behind him.

Hunter tucked the radio in this web belt, and hooked the clip on the handle of the handset to his chinstrap, with the mike close to his ear. This way he could hear the very soft tone of the radio if anyone called. I'm red two now, he thought. It was cool being in charge, he loved it. Twenty minutes went by quickly, so quickly that Hunter had to check his watch as he heard the sound of footsteps creeping up, just over the sound of the rain. "Could this be them already?" Hunter moved slowly to a knee, his weapon pulled tight into his shoulder. His left hand holding up the front of his machine gun, and the butt of a flashlight. He didn't turn it on; he would wait for them to give a signal. If they were close but couldn't exactly locate the rest of the squad, they would flash the dull red light; Hunter in turn would flash his light back to facilitate the link up. If they walked up on his position, Hunter would verbally stop them and challenge them with the password.

The steps grew closer; Hunter could see a form emerge from the inky blackness of the triple canopy. In his night vision, it looked like a darker green blob moving out of a sheet of speckled lighter green.

"Halt," Hunter whispered, as the form approached his position. Hunter's finger just above the trigger of his weapon, barrel trained on the figures chest. The form stopped. "Snow."

"Farm," the figure returned. Hunter recognized Sergeant Frost's voice.

"Enter," Hunter responded.

There were three people in the group now, they had put the M-60 Machine Gun crew in place and were now returning to pick the rest up.

Henry moved into the perimeter and knelt beside Hunter. "Ok, we found a pretty good spot for the ambush about 75 meters to our front, at about your ten o'clock. The 60's in a great position at a bend in the road, he's got good fields of fire down both ways of the path. We're gonna set up on the northern most part of the road, just like we talked about in the OP order. We've got some good concealment in some heavy underbrush along the road. We're moving in about 2 mikes (minutes)."

Henry stood and went to Lancaster to give him the same information. When the transfer was complete, he moved to the next individual in the line. A minute later he was back at Hunter's spot. "Let's go."

Hunter stood and followed, looking behind to make sure Lancaster was following. After a few meters the path dipped down in a small gully. Henry made a sharp left turn at the bottom, and proceeded forward for about 25 meters. He then stopped and took a knee. Hunter and Lancaster did the same.

"This is it," he whispered, gesturing up the incline. "Remember; don't open up until the claymores go off. Hunter, don't set your claymore off until Sgt. Frost blows his. Then wax those bastards. Any questions?"

Both Hunter and Lancaster shook their heads.

"Hunter, I'm going to put you in first. Lancaster, stay here."

Henry and Hunter stood, Hunter leading the way up the side of the hill. They crept slowly up, every step slow and deliberate, so not to make a sound. Hunter could make out an opening in the jungle canopy several meters in front of his squad leader. The opening let the star light flow onto the muddy trail that cut through the jungle. As they approached, Henry dropped and began to crawl, Hunter did the same. The rain, that had actually let up to almost a sprinkle always helped in this type of a situation. It's hard to hear small noises when it's raining. It drowns out footsteps at more than a few meters. As they approached, the vegetation thickened. In the places that opened up for the sun, a large growth of underbrush and small plants flourished. Soon they were only two meters from the road.

"This is it," Henry said in a barely audible voice. "Your sector of fire is from that tree," pointing across the trail to a large tree a Hunter's two o'clock, "to there," pointing at another tree at his ten o'clock. "Don't set up your Claymore until I get Lancaster into place, so you know where he is. I'm putting him in there" pointing just to the right of where they currently lay, "and I'm going to be there," pointing to the left.

Hunter nodded.

Henry turned and crawled back in the direction they had just come from.

CHAPTER 16

Consciousness came slowly. First it was the sounds of the jungle, although there was a ringing in his ears - a constant hum that sounded like a high pitched mosquito hovering outside his ear. The sounds seemed to be muted. The vision came next; Emil opened his eyes to darkness. Pure darkness. *Am I blind?* He wondered.

Next came the sensation of weight pushing down on every part of his body. It felt as if he weighed 500 pounds. Each time he would attempt to move a body part, he was met with resistance. *Am I dead?*

As his senses returned, a huge pounding in his head became noticeable.

He moved his right hand. The motion came without restraint. In the heap of debris that was left of the bunker, the slight movement of a hand became apparent.

The foggy moments before he lost consciousness began to play through his mind like a slow motion movie. *There was a massive explosion . . .* he lifted his right forearm, it also moved freely . . . *then everything went black . . .* he lifted his elbow up and planted his hand and pushed with all his might. Emil's right shoulder emerged from the pile of sand bags and rubble that was once the bunker. He screamed at the top of his lungs as he forced his upper body from the layer that covered him. His body broke free, and he stood on wobbly knees. *The fucking American Pigs would pay for this!*

In the sparse light, Emil surveyed the area. The area that had been the mortar pit was now really a pit. Nothing remained in the spot that had once held the mortar tube except for a three foot deep hole with remnants of sandbags scattered along its sides. The mound of remains that he now stood on was what was left of the bunker where he had his ear repaired earlier in the day.

"Fernando?" Emil squeaked in a horse voice. He glanced to his left.

From the corner of his eye Emil could just made out Fernando's face, covered in dirt only ten feet away from where he was standing on the downhill side of the pile. *He must have been buried too!* Emil scurried across the carnage of the bunker to reach his friend.

"Fernando, FERNANDO!"

Fernando appeared to be positioned on his back with debris covering him from the chest down. "Fernando!" he called again.

Fernando didn't move or open his eyes.

Emil reached behind Fernando's head to lift him from his confines. A stickiness covered his hand as he began to lift. Fernando's scalp gave way and the skin peeled from his head forward, distorting the features of his once taut facial structure. At that same moment Fernando's upper torso moved forward under the pressure from behind his head. The head and chest rolling forward and over onto his face, the body had been completely severed midway through his trunk.

"AY DIOS MIO!" Emil screamed.

CHAPTER 17

Hunter surveyed the area as he unfolded the bipod legs from the front of his SAW. He could clearly see down both directions of the trail, both of which veered off in different directions. *The M-60 Machine Gun crew had to be in there*, he thought as he watched the area where the trail turned north to his right. He concentrated his nods in that area to look for indications of the crew. After a minute or so with no indication of a presence, he decided that they were very well hidden. He heard a slight rustle in the underbrush to his right rear – it was Henry and Lancaster.

As he strained his eyes to peer through the underbrush, he could see movement between the labyrinth of plant life. He could just make out the dark silhouette of a hand as the movement stopped. Henry was giving him his sectors of fire. A few seconds later, he could see Henry slip back into the jungle.

It was time to set in his Claymore. His heart began to race again. If someone came walking down the trail, he would be caught in the open, essentially defenseless. The key would be to do it quickly, without making any noise. Hunter pulled the bag that contained the mine and accessories from his shoulder and placed it in front of his face. He knew that Lancaster, and the rest of the squad would be covering him. "What if the M-60 Machine Gun crew think I'm an LBG coming down the trail?" he thought in an instant of doubt. "No, they know that we're setting in Claymores, it'll be fine."

Holding the Claymore bag in his left hand, and his weapon in his right, he slowly moved forward on his stomach - low crawling toward the trail. Hunter stopped at a small tree, just at the trail's edge. "This is a good spot," he thought. "The blast of the mine covered a large portion of the trail, while the tree would serve to block a large portion of the back-blast when the mine was detonated."

Hunter set his weapon just in front of him as he pulled the actual mine from the bag. He folded out the two sets of scissor-like legs. Next, he extracted the wire and the blasting cap. He unscrewed one of the wells on top of the mine, inserted the blasting cap, routed the wire through the plug that he had just removed, and screwed the plug back in. He looked up and scanned down both directions of the trail. Hunter then placed the mine directly in front of the tree, facing the curved side toward the trail. That was one of the things Hunter had found interesting when he was first introduced to the Claymore. The curved front side of the mine actually had the words "Front Toward Enemy," on it. I guess they wanted to make sure no one turned the thing in the wrong direction. It was too dark to make out the words, but Hunter could feel the letters. He knew which way it went anyway; he had had a ton of training on mines, both in regular training and in advanced demolition school.

Hunter pushed the scissor-like feet into the soft ground in front of the tree. He then reached over and grabbed some leaves from the opposite side of the tree, being careful not to make the ground look as though it had been disturbed, and covered the mine. He then took his weapon and sat it to his right rear, parallel with his knee and ankle. As he slid backward on his stomach, he unraveled the cord from the spool, which was now attached to the Claymore. When his head was next to his weapon, he repeated the process until he was in the original position that Sergeant Henry had put him in. He was about fifteen feet from the Claymore. He extracted the clacker and the test kit from the bag, unrolled the rest of the wire, and prepared to test the system.

The Claymore mine is a very soldier friendly mine. It's easy to use, very effective, and easy to test. It was the testing part that always made Hunter a little nervous. It was just the matter of plugging in a testing device into the wire coming from the mine, and plugging in the other side to the clacker that set the mine off. When the clacker was squeezed, the test module had a small light that would flash red. The system worked by sending a small amount of current through the wire, including the blasting cap, to ensure there was a complete circuit. The amount of juice through the system was less than was required to activate the cap. Hunter always wondered if all the caps were made the same way, wondered if some might go off with less juice.

Hunter removed the rubber protective end caps from the testing device and plugged in the wire that went to the mine. He then removed the plug on the clacker, and plugged it into the opposite side of the tester. *He mentally went through the process again, "mines pointing in the right direction, caps in the mine, retaining cap is screwed in tight, back-blast area is clear, wire is run into the test module, module into the clacker. OK, it's right.* He looked up and down the trail again, there was no one. Hunter removed his nods, and looked down at his clacker and tester. *Ok, here we go.* He removed the safety on the activation device and inadvertently held his breath. He squeezed the clacker in one swift motion. It made, what seemed to be in this environment, a loud click. The light on the tester flashed. An inaudible sigh escaped his mouth. It was ready. He replaced the safety on the clacker, removed the tester, and plugged the clacker directly into the wire. The system was ready to fire.

Hunter settled into a position behind his gun, so he could pivot over his entire sector. But there was a problem, with a slightly uphill angle, the barrel of his SAW was pointing too high in the kill zone of the ambush area. He reached forward to his bipod legs, and lowered each of them downward. As he returned to his firing position, he pulled the butt tight into his shoulder. "That looks better," he thought as he sighted down the length of the gun. He rolled slightly to his side and grabbed his night vision, replacing them on the head mount. Peering into the area through the enhanced vision verified his gun's elevation.

He held the clacker in his left hand, and began scanning the area. After a few minutes he turned the nods off to conserve batteries. Hunter left them on the head harness, but pushed them up on his head, so they wouldn't obstruct his vision. "I'll just use them to scan the area periodically, or if I hear or see something," he thought.

The waiting began. It always happened this way on ambush. You sit for hours and hours, then maybe the enemy would come along, or maybe he wouldn't. The rain finally stopped. Hunter was completely soaked; every piece of his body was wet. The wet really isn't that big of a deal when you're moving, but when you're stationary it can suck the heat right out of you. You could be cold in the 80 degree heat of the jungle.

As the first, second, and third, hours floated by, Hunter began to fight sleep. He had very little sleep in the past two days. One second he would be looking down the kill zone, the next his head would bob downward. He would then catch himself, and will himself to stay awake.

I wonder if I will get into Heaven, with the people I have already killed on record, Hunter thought. *I can see it now, Saint Peter rejecting me at the entrance of the pearly gates. It will be like the cadence we sing when were running. "When I get to Heaven, Saint Peters gonna say, How'd you earn your livin' boy, how'd you earn your pay? I'll reply with a whole lot of anger, Made my liv'in as an Airborne Ranger!" Only the next part will be Saint Peter booting your ass because you have blood on your hands. God has to forgive you for things like that, Right?*

Hunter looked at his watch, it was 04:20. They had been in position for over seven hours already. "The op order said that we will pull out at 07:00 if we have negative contact," he thought. Just as he looked up, a shadow caught his eye. His heart seemed to stand still, as he held his breath. There was something moving on the trail, on his right, just in front of where the 60 position was. Hunter slowly moved his hand up to turn on his nods; he pulled them down in front of his eyes in one smooth motion. "There they are," he thought. There were four silhouettes moving down the road toward him, three carrying AK-47's, one carrying what looked like a 60 mm mortar tube on his shoulder. More came around the bend in the trail. Hunter could make out the base plate for the mortar on the back of one of the individuals coming around the corner.

Hunter's heart began to race, the adrenalin flowing through his veins. "This is it, this is it, this is it," kept going through his mind. He could hear muffled voices in Spanish as they approached his position. He consciously controlled his breathing; he quietly moved the safety on the Claymore clacker. He almost switched his weapon, before he remembered the sound that it made, "they'll hear the click. I'll wait til' I hit the Claymore."

Hunter rabidly moved his eyes back and forth along the road, to assess the situation, and decide which targets he would engage first in his kill zone. The first two were rapidly approaching Hunter, they were only feet away. "*Blow the Claymore, Blow the Claymore*" he screamed in his mind. The front two passed. "We can't let them out of the kill zone; we can't let them out of the kill zone." The pressure to activate the clacker weighed heavily on his hand. "Come on, COME ON!"

BOOOOOM.

The Claymore from Sergeant Frost fired. Hunter squeezed the clacker with all his might. Instinctively closing his eyes.

BOOOOM.

There was a large flash as the mine exploded. The fiery of hell was unleashed in a split second. Weapons opened up into the kill zone, with the M-60 tracer rounds running up and down the length of the trail from their position on at the bend.

Hunter pulled the trigger and swept his kill zone. The flashes from the Claymores had made the night vision momentarily useless. He rapidly moved his nods up, and continued raking the area. He paused after a few seconds. A whistle resonated through the jungle; it was the cease fire signal. Hunter pulled his night vision back down, they were now starting to clear up. The solid green that had been created from the intense light, was now settling out into discernable shapes. Hunter moved up to his knees and folded the bipod legs of his SAW up, in anticipation of the double whistle.

When the assault through signal, double whistle was given, he would run through the kill zone and eliminate any hostiles that were missed in the initial fire.

In a way it was pretty amazing, what the training had done. Things that would petrify a normal person, flowed naturally for Hunter. It was more like someone flying on autopilot. Do what needs to be done, do it quickly, properly, with viciousness.

Two sharp whistle blasts rang out through the night. Hunter sprang to his feet and lurched forward. He rapidly moved over the trail, stepping through the maze of tangled bodies that littered the area. Lancaster appeared to his right and Henry to his left. They moved in a parallel line as they assaulted through the kill zone. He could hear shots from his immediate right. Nothing was moving in his area. Once on the opposite side of the trail, he took a knee and began scanning for hostiles. The smell of gunpowder and blood was thick in the night. On the trail he could hear wheezing from someone who had been hit. As Hunter turned to survey the path of broken human debris, the sound stopped. The loud roar of the jungle, which had seemed to break to listen to the firefight, resumed; first with a few birds, then with the entire host of players in the night.

CHAPTER 18

Emil ran down a path in the jungle, away from the compound. It was still very dark; he had no idea what time it was. There was no telling how long he had been out. The coagulated blood from behind Fernando's head was already cool when he had touched it. That seemed like a good indication that he had been out for awhile. He didn't know where he was going to go yet, he only knew he had to get away and regroup. So he ran down a path that he could just barely make out in the darkness, periodically slamming into vegetation on either side of the walk way.

"*I could go to the Lab, I can meet my compadres there, and we can attack these bastards,*" Emil thought as he stopped to take a breath.

From somewhere up the trail two almost simultaneous explosions rang out, followed by the sounds of a firefight. "*Judging from the sounds, the gun battle must be a good kilometer or two up the trail*", Emil contemplated. He recognized the rhythmic sounds of an M-60 machine gun, punctuated with pops from small arms fire. "*Judging from the volume of fire, there must be a lot of weapons firing at the same thing*". The cacophony of sound radiated through the jungle for ten seconds, and then ended as quickly as it had started.

Emil stood for a moment, waiting to see if the gunfire was over. He then continued his quest down the trail. "*Maybe my compadres have ambushed some of those American pigs at the Lab,*" he thought as he continued to move. The only problem with that idea was the fact that the small arms fire sounded like M-16 rounds, he knew that most of the guards at the Lab carried AK-74s. He forced the idea out of his mind and staggered on down the intermittently moon lit path.

CHAPTER 19

The third whistle rang out in the night. Hunter knew this was the signal for the POW search team and casualty collection teams to rake over the bodies, to look for Intel and survivors. It was his cue. In all the turmoil, he had forgotten that he was on the search team until the second the whistle had blown.

Hunter rose to his feet and scrambled along the path to his right, in the direction the patrol had come from. The op order said that they would start the search in front of the 60's position. When he reached the end, Sergeant Frost was kneeling in the middle of the road with Corry, from B team who was already there. He quickly slid on his knee beside them.

It would have been obvious that it was Corry, even if Hunter didn't know he was the one who was supposed to be there. Corry had all the facial features you would associate with a mafia Don – the prominent jaw and forehead, strong cheekbones, olive skin, and piercing dark eyes. He was of average height, but was built like a brick shithouse and strong as an ox. The facial features, even through the face paint, and the size identified him quickly.

"Make sure you check those fuckers good," Sergeant Frost whispered in a elevated tone. "Remember to check for grenades first, got it?"

Hunter and Corry nodded simultaneously.

"Hurry up, everyone for ten clicks had to have heard us."

Hunter and Corry moved to the first body in the path, each kneeling on either side.

"You want to search, or cover first?" Corry asked.

"I'll search, just make sure you cover my ass," Hunter responded.

Hunter sat down his SAW and unsnapped his night vision goggles and allowed them to hang down, he then tucked them under one side of he web belt harness. The man was faced down. He was wearing American style jungle BDUs with no helmet. His weapon was lodged underneath him.

Corry took up a prone position opposite of Hunter. The procedure involved Hunter pulling the individual up on his side, Corry would look to make sure there were no loose grenades and that the man didn't have a weapon. He would then say "clear." Hunter would continue to flip the person over and check his entire person for any information.

Hunter grabbed the man's shoulder facing Corry. It was warm, he knew this was a living breathing human being a moment before, but he just wasn't expecting the body to be so warm. He pulled skyward.

Hunter could feel a jerk in the guy's body has he lifted. "OH MY GOD, HE'S NOT DEAD!" Consumed his mind in a wave of panic.

The man rolled toward Hunter.

A monstrous sound rang in the night. "CRACK!"

A wave of wetness hit Hunter in the face and neck with great stinging force. He felt as if someone had slapped him in the face with a wet towel. The taste of iron permeated his mouth, slightly filling it with a grainy substance, almost like sand in jelly.

Hunter fell backwards onto his back. It was as if the world had gone into slow motion again. The brilliant flash of light that had accompanied the sound seemed to overcome all that he saw. His eyes were burning, and the massive sound seemed to hold on in a constant echo that kept ringing on forever. "*He must have had a grenade*" was the only semblance of cognitive thought that ran through his mind.

As the bright light faded, the star filled sky came into focus. "*Hey, the rain clouds went away.*" Hunter was then aware of a shaped moving over top of him. The figure got closer and closer, until he was directly in his face. It was Sergeant Frost. He could see his lips moving, but the ringing wouldn't let him discern what was being said. The ringing began to die down, as the garbled words became clear.

"Are you OK?" Sergeant Frost asked, the concern painted in the features of his camouflaged face.

Hunter nodded. He began to speak, but his mouth was clogged with something. He turned his head and spit.

Everything seemed to feel OK. He turned and spit again. "Yeah, I'm OK."

"God damn it!" the words would have been screams in any other environment, but he had pulled the sound level down to a whisper. Sergeant Frost was pissed. "You scared the fuck out of me, you little shit head!"

Hunter turned and spit again, as he pulled himself onto a knee. He looked at the LBG. The man was now on his side with a small part of his head missing. It finally occurred to him what had happened. Corry had shot the guy in the head when he tried to flip over. The shit in his mouth was the man's blood and brains.

"Are you sure you're not hit?" Sergeant Frost asked again. "Wash that shit off your face and out of your mouth."

Hunter took one of his canteens from his web belt. He knelt down and popped the strap on his K-pot, removing his helmet. Opening his canteen, he poured some water in his mouth and bent his head sideways to pour the water over his face. He swished the water around and spat again. He used both hands to wash off his face.

Sergeant Frost had grabbed Lancaster from the line, he and Corry continued the search that was started just a moment before.

The ringing in Hunter's ears seemed to be dying down, more like the buzz of high power wires now, instead of the deafening roar that had once invaded his ears. He poured some of the water in his helmet, and scrubbed off the outer rim, then poured out the remainder on the ground. He washed his mouth out two more times, and wiped his eyes with the dew rag that he had in his pocket. "That's better," he thought. He took the remaining water from his canteen and drank in down in three large gulps. He put his K-pot back on, and shook his head, as if to remove some of the cobwebs that still remained.

"You alright?" Sergeant Frost asked again.

"Roger Sergeant," Hunter was finally feeling back to normal. *If you could ever feel normal after some shit like that,* he thought.

Corry and Lancaster were already on their way back from the search. They took a knee directly in front of Sergeant Frost and Hunter.

"Sergeant, we found this on one of the LBGs," Lancaster said as he handed a square piece of paper to Sergeant Frost. "It's a map."

Sergeant Frost quickly grabbed his red lens flashlight. "Bring it in tight."

The group of four made a very tight circle, to block as much of the red light as possible. As Sergeant Frost unfolded the map, it was clear there was writing in several of the areas. "Here we are," he pointed with the end of a blade of grass that he picked up off the ground. About an inch north on the map of where he was pointing, was a small circle with two smaller circles on either side. It appeared to be just off of the trail that they were on. "That's it, that's the fucking camp and drug storage area," he said as he moved the makeshift pointer to the circles. He switched off the light. "Ok, get back to your teams and get ready to move. We're moving out to a rally point 50 meters north of this position."

Hunter cautiously crept to this position on the North side of the road. The taste in his mouth and the smell that filled his head was horrible, like a combination of raw hamburger and rust. On his way, he replaced his nods on his head harness and turned them on. As he reached his spot, Henry was moving toward him.

"What the fuck happened?" Henry asked.

"One of those little fuckers wasn't dead. . . . when I turned him over. . . he went for a weapon. . . or something. Corry splattered his head all over me," Hunter replied.

"Shit, you OK?"

"Yeah, I'm good. I've got a little bit of a headache, and a nasty ass taste in my mouth."

"You don't smell too good either, damn. The bugs are going to be all over your ass tonight," Henry said, trying to make light of the situation.

Sergeant Henry's radio sprung into action, in a very low hum. Henry pulled the hand mic closer to his ear to listen.

Hunter could just make out bits and pieces, with the volume so low – not to mention the ringing in his ears. "It sounds like we're doing a follow on mission," he thought.

"Roger, Out," Henry responded as he keyed the mic. He leaned in Lancaster's direction and made a low clicking noise to get his attention. When Lancaster looked over, Henry waved him in.

Lancaster came over and moved in next to Hunter.

Sergeant Henry took out his canteen and took a drink. "Get ready to move, we're going to a rally point about 50 meters north of here for a frag o. . . . We're going after that drug lab."

CHAPTER 20

"We're on point," Sergeant Henry said as he stood. "Hunter, head on a three two zero for 50 meters. Keep your eyes open."

Hunter pulled his compass from its pouch on his web belt along with his small Maglight. He cupped the red lens flashlight around the compass, leaving a small opening at the top so he could see the dial. Rotating the bezel ring, he set the heading on the compass for 320 magnetic.

Henry tapped Hunter on the shoulder and pointed, motioning for him to move out. Hunter held his compass with his left hand and the pistol grip of his machine gun with his right. He oriented himself in the proper direction and began to move.

The jungle was thick for the first several feet, and then it opened up with several small pathways. Hunter got on a small path that went in the general direction and began to move. As he counted his pace, he kept track of the direction that he was drifting off his heading. In this case it was slightly to the left. At the end of his 500 meter pace count, he knew that he would have to move back to the right several meters to get back on track.

As Hunter moved, the rest of the squad fell into a single file behind him. When Hunter reached his designated point 50 meters in, he took a knee. It seemed a little strange for Hunter to only make a 50 meter move. Most of the time after an ambush, or any engagement for that matter, they would move hundreds of meters away as soon as possible. In fact, the op order had originally had the squad pulling back 50 meters after the ambush. *Sergeant Frost must not want to move us too close to the drug lab.* That would be bad, running up on an outpost that was surely ready and waiting after all the noise they had just made.

As the rest of the squad members reached the location, Sergeant Henry pointed out positions in a circle to form a tight 360 degree perimeter. When Sergeant Frost reached the center with Hunter and Henry, Henry tapped

Hunter's shoulder and pointed to a position in the circle. Hunter went to his new post, and slowly slid into a prone position.

"The smell almost went away," Hunter thought. He could still smell the sweet pungent odors of the jungle, but not quite as well as before. It seemed he tasted the raw meat like smell, more than the differentiating odor. It seemed like it had already begun to rot, with just a tinge of the aromatic bodies that were left in the hot sun that he had encountered the day before.

Hunter searched the area with his nods. On a tree, not more that fifteen meters to his front left, he could see a slow undulating movement. The movement caught him off guard at first, causing him to pull his weapon in tight with his thumb instantly putting pressure on his selector switch. "*It's a snake*," he thought as he surveyed the movement. "It's a big fucking snake." The shape was moving up the side of a tree, from the looks of it. It had to be at least six or seven feet long. He switched off his night vision to conserve the batteries, unhooking them from the head harness. A second later, his eyes adjusted back to the darkness.

"The canopy must not be so thick here," Hunter noted as he looked around. He could clearly make out shapes. Looking up, he could see that the roof of the trees was notably thinner for a large area directly in front of his position. He looked at his watch, 0510. It would be BMNT in about an hour and a half. BMNT (Before Morning Nautical Twilight) is the time before the sun comes up, but it starts getting light.

A minute later, Henry walked up behind him, and knelt at his side. "The drug lab was only about 650 meters from here, according to their map. They have two LPOPs, one directly north of their position, the other directly south. We are going to head on a 350 degree azimuth for 600 meters, then turn to 95 degrees for 30 meters. That will take us to that same trail we were on; the objective is twenty meters on the other side of the trail. We will be on high ground on this side of the trail, that's where we are going to put the 60 in. We are going to loop around to the left and take out the northern LPOP (Listening Post, Observation Post) as the 60 opens up on the lab. We will assault through the outpost, straight through the main objective. The 60 will lift and shift fire to their right when we pop green smoke. Donaldson, from the 60 team will engage the southern LPOP when we hit the one to the north. As the 60 shifts fire, they will take out anything that is left. We have to get moving, so we can hit them at dawn. Any questions?"

Hunter shook his head.

Henry moved to the next person in the circle to transfer the information. As Henry moved away, Hunter could see Sergeant Singer on the other side of the perimeter, giving the same speech to his team. Hunter pulled his compass out again, and put the new heading on the dial.

Several minutes later, Sergeant Frost moved next to Hunter, in the same spot that Henry had occupied. "Keep a close eye out; we don't know how many of those little fuckers are running around here. We don't want to be compromised before we hit these bastards. Especially after you make that turn, if you don't watch it you'll run right up on them. You know where you're going?"

Hunter nodded.

"Let's get these fuckers," with that statement, Sergeant Frost pointed in the direction of travel and moved back.

Hunter took a knee, snapped his night vision back on, and glanced over his shoulder. Henry was just walking forward. He nodded, and Hunter began to move.

The movement was very easy. A small path followed his azimuth almost exactly. As he walked, Hunter's heart began to race again, the pounding in his ears almost overpowered the ringing.

"It looks clear," he thought as he moved every few steps. After a step or two Hunter would scan the entire area, and look to the rear to make sure that he didn't lose the guy behind him.

A hundred meters went uneventfully, then two hundred, then three. Soon he had completed his 600 meter leg. As he did, he stopped and gave the signal for everyone to take a knee. The squad went down as if they were doing the wave at a football game.

Hunter took a deep breath, unhooking his goggles. He retrieved his flashlight, and made the adjustment on his compass. Every movement was very slow and deliberate; any noise at this point could compromise the mission, or cost someone their life. Henry moved up by his side and handed him his canteen.

Hunter took a long drink and handed it back. He put his goggles back on as Henry drank the remainder of his canteen and put it away. Hunter glanced at his watch, 0610. The first rays of sunlight were now showing in the sky.

"Let's kick some ass," Hunter whispered in a barely audible whisper.

Sergeant Henry patted him on the shoulder and nodded.

Hunter began to move on his 95 degree heading. He immediately started up an incline. "This is good," he thought, "I'm in the right place."

Twenty-five meters by his pace count, he had crested the ridge. In a blast of excitement, he could see the trail spring from the jungle on the downward slope. And on the other side of the trail, several lights from the compound were dancing in the jungle.

Hunter lifted his fist slowly in the air, the signal for freeze. The steps that he could hear behind him instantaneously stopped. He turned his fist sideways, flattening out his hand, and motioned to the ground. Everyone in the patrol slowly moved to the prone position on the ground.

Through his nods, Hunter could clearly see the compound and both LPOPs. Individuals in both of the outposts were smoking. *"How fucking stupid is that,"* he thought. . There was a sound too, it couldn't quite make it out at first, and then it clicked "Generator. They have a generator running, that's how they have the lights. They may not have even heard that ambush."

Sergeant Frost, Sergeant Henry, and Sergeant Singer appeared to Hunter's side. After all four had surveyed the situation visually for a few minutes, Hunter could see Sergeant Frost motion. He silently tapped Henry, and then made a looping motion with his finger to the rear then around, pausing momentarily just on this side of the outpost, then pointed to the LPOP on the left. Then he raised a second finger, together with the first, and swept his hand through the compound.

Henry gave him the thumbs up. Sergeant Frost turned to look at Singer. He too gave the thumbs up sign.

Henry grabbed Hunter's leg as he rose to a crouch. As Hunter looked, he nodded to the rear. Hunter followed.

A few steps back, Hunter could see the M-60 machine gun team. Henry stopped momentarily, and motioned forward toward Sergeant Frost. The team picked up and moved forward to get into their over watch position for the assault.

Hunter followed his team leader, as they moved back to loop around and assault the LPOP first. As they passed each individual in the patrol, lying along their original route, Henry gently tapped them and gave the hand signal to "follow".

After they had moved another fifteen meters, they again halted to wait for Sergeant Frost and Sergeant Singer. With the "halt signal", all took a knee on the side of the trail.

Hunter's heart rate began to increase again. It still seemed so strange to him, still like a dream. Everything was numb. He felt things, but it was more like he was feeling through someone else. As he moved along, it often felt like he was watching himself, instead of being himself.

The darkness was noticeably starting to recede. *"We're going to have to get into position soon!"* Hunter thought, again glancing at his watch. *"In twenty-five more minutes the sun will be up."*

Sergeant Frost came up the small trail between the squad, walking briskly. As he approached, he motioned forward.

Henry stood, as did the rest of the patrol in a rapid accordion movement. He moved out, making a large loop that would take us up on line with the Listening and Observation Post.

"We've got to be getting close," Hunter thought with each step as they crept toward the enemy. Soon, Hunter could see the crest of the ridge. A few steps further, he saw the large trail, and the enemy. His heart was racing again.

Henry gave the "freeze" signal. Hunter stopped, not even breathing.

Sergeant Henry slowly turned, with his left hand he used two fingers to point at his eyes, and then at the soldier standing twenty feet away.

"*Security. . . Cover him,*" Hunter now understood what he meant. He cautiously moved to the side of where Henry was, keeping the barrel of his SAW trained on the shadowy figure. In the background he could hear the generator.

Hunter could hear the quiet footsteps of his squad approaching from the rear. Henry was putting them on line on either side of Hunter. When they assaulted across, it would be very important to stay on line, that was a lesson he learned early in his training when he almost got shot in a live fire exercise. Hunter glanced for a split second to his left and right. Everyone was spaced out about five feet apart.

CHAPTER 21

"WHAM," Emil hit the ground hard. He had been walking down the trail at a very brisk pace when he tripped over something, something solid in the middle of the path. He was immediately aware of the metallic smell of blood on the air.

Emil pushed himself up on his hands. He propped his knees on the squashy log he had just tripped over. Reaching downward to feel the log, his hand pressed into what felt like a bowl of warm Jello. The realization hit him, it wasn't a log. It was a body from the firefight he had heard a few minutes before.

"PUNTA!" he screamed.

He stood and began to run. "WHAM," he fell again. Stumbling forward he tripped again. He crawled forward on his hands and knees as fast as he could. "Wham," he fell over another corpse as his arms folded under his own body, his face plowing into the ground.

CHAPTER 22

The sky was really starting to get light. As Hunter watched, the enemy soldier casually strolled into the small sand bagged area, his full upper half still in clear view. He could just make out the top of another one's head; it looked like they were talking. The butterflies were back in full force in his stomach.

The sunlight was coming fast. Hunter quickly unsnapped his night vision goggles, and pulled the cord off from around his neck, never taking his eyes off the men in the small bunker. He quickly unbuttoned the side cargo pocket of his pants and placed them inside, fastening the buttons afterward.

"It's almost dawn," Hunter thought as a bead of sweat ran down his face. "The 60's opening up at dawn, it should be in a minute! Remember, don't move across the compound until we throw green smoke." The thought kept repeating in his head, it seemed quicker and quicker with each run through. He raised his SAW from his waist to his shoulder, pulling it in tight. "Breath control. Breath control." Each breath seemed to be quicker than the last, causing the sights to move up and down. He consciously slowed it down. The man was directly in his sight picture. "I got em', I got em', I got em'."

The rhythmic popping of the M-60 broke into the sounds of the night; tracers began to rain down on the compound 30 meters on the other side of the LPOP.

With the first "pop", Hunter flipped his selector switch off of the safety position, and pulled the trigger.

"Buzzzzit," Hunter could see the tracers from his barrel streak in a straight line through the man. The force of blow forced his body to violently flip backwards. As Hunter finished his first burst, he could hear the fire from all in his squad. The tracers were pummeling the entire area that the LPOP occupied.

"GO!" Sergeant Henry's voice rang out between the nearly constant pops of gun fire.

Hunter stood and moved forward, watching the post and the jungle beyond. As he reached the trail, he rapidly glanced left and right. "*They're on line, they're on line!*" He ran across the trail, pointing his weapon into the circle of sandbags. Buzzzzzit. He sprayed the area, and then looked forward. There was a slight open area down a small ravine, up on the other side through some sparse vegetation he could see the tents, and enemy troops running around wildly.

Hunter hesitated for a second, spraying the area with lead, from one end to the other. From the high ground on his right, he could see the tracers raining down on the area. "*Watch your ammo, Watch your ammo*", he thought as he sprayed another burst. With a loud crack a tracer flew just to his left, he glanced left and right again. "Fuck, I'm not on line!"

Moving his attention back to the compound, he identified a man running in his direction. Buzzzzzzzzit. The man's momentum from the decline made him twist to the side and roll down the ravine, twenty meters in front of Hunter. He looked left and right again, everyone was coming back on line.

Hunter resumed his upright position and moved forward with the group. The M-60 Machine Gun was still hammering away as they reached the bottom of the small six foot deep ravine. From his left, he saw a large object float through the air toward the compound. A second later he heard the distinctive "pop" of a smoke canister going off. A bellowing green cloud of smoke began to rise skyward. The sound from the line seemed to stop for a moment, the only sounds of fire radiated from the compound and M-60.

Hunter looked to his left to see Brady, back to his right to see Sergeant Henry. There was a short break in the M-60 fire.

"He's shifting fire," Hunter thought. He started up the incline, making sure the others were moving from the corner of his eye. As he crested the incline, the entire compound came into view. There were two green tents side by side, woven through the openings in the trees to his eleven o'clock, about twenty meters away. Between the two was the small generator. Four bodies were scattered in front of the opening in the tent on the left. Directly in front of him, twenty meters away was a long, thin shelter house looking structure with one long table in the center. Camouflage netting was draped over the top, and down the opposite side in several places. A thick hedge of jungle fell between the right end of the structure and the trail. A man sprung from this patch of green and ran toward the tents, his AK-47 leading his charge. Two or three steps into his dash, a hail of lead hit him from several angles as the squad advanced on line, his body jerking in several different directions at once.

"*He looks like a puppet,*" was the first thing that went through Hunter's mind, as he turned toward the tents. The line of Rangers was advancing across the objective very quickly. Hunter quickly aimed at the generator. Buzzzzzit. The sound trailed off as sparks flew from the impact of the rounds.

Hunter moved to the right of the shelter house to avoid the netting. He noticed large white blocks of something stacked on the tables as he rounded the corner.

Henry double tapped the body of the man that had been the rag doll just moments before as they swept past his body. Looking to his left, he could see people entering the tents – shots ringing out as they disappeared inside. They had almost reached the opposite end of the compound; where a very large rubber tree introduced the dense jungle again.

Sergeant Henry moved to the left side of the tree, Hunter only five meters to his left. As Hunter glanced past Henry to the area directly behind the tree, he could see him. The world stopped and went into slow motion. It was the enemy.

The man surged from the respite of a notch in the tree. His barrel moving forward as his dirty brown face screamed in hate, taking Henry completely off guard.

CHAPTER 23

Hunter swung his body, SAW leading the way in the direction of the attacker. Falling from the combination of the centrifugal force of his movement and the violent turn, he pulled the trigger of his weapon.

Buzzzzzit.

The tracers whizzed inches in front of Henry, impacting the man's neck and head.

The head exploded in a massive mist of red and gray as the body fell forward, knocking Henry to the ground.

As Hunter hit the ground he rolled and sprung back to his feet. In one giant leap he reached his team leader and pulled the dead man off of him in one sweep as he grabbed the back of the man's LBE (Belt that carries his equipment).

"ARE YOU OK?" Hunter screamed into Henry's blood soaked face.

Henry's response was instant, "GO!"

Hunter turned and ran in his original direction of travel until he was five meters into the jungle's edge. There he dove to the ground in a prone position behind his SAW, searching for targets. The popping of the 60 stopped. "He must have cleared that other LPOP, or ran out of ammo," he thought.

A second later, he caught a glance of Henry plopping down five meters to his right.

Hunter glanced down at his ammo; there were only two rounds visible outside the feet tray. "Holy shit, I'm about out of ammo," he thought. He turned to Henry, "Cover me, I need to change drums."

"Go, hurry up," Henry barked back.

Hunter rapidly turned on his left side, reached down and unsnapped his SAW pouch on his LBE. In one swift motion he extracted the dark green plastic drum of ammo and set it next to his weapon. Opening his feed tray, he unhooked the empty drum and grabbed the remaining rounds.

Snapping the new drum into place, he reached in the new reservoir of ammo and grabbed the end of the belt of 5.56 rounds. Next he draped the rounds across the feed tray into place and holding them with his right hand, shut the tray with his left. He pulled the charging handle back, extracting the round that was in the chamber, and let it slide forward, allowing the bolt to lock a round into place. He placed the remaining rounds into the SAW pouch on his LBE, snapped it shut and flew behind his gun. "Ready."

The fire had died down to nothing. In the movement around the long building, Hunter and Henry had become separated from the rest of the squad. They both sat and listened.

Fifteen or twenty meters to the left, Hunter could hear steps then a distinct thud as someone plopped on the ground in the prone position. "It's probably Brady," he thought. A second later he heard a distinct "click, click," sound. It was Brady. The clicking sound was what Rangers in his platoon would always make to get each others attention without speaking in the bush. Hunter clicked back. Henry looked over and nodded, then tilted his head in that direction, indicating to move that way.

Hunter clicked again, just to be sure he knew it was him, then stood in a low crouch and moved toward the sound. As he moved, he saw Brady. When he was five meters away, still having visual contact, he again went into the prone position. Henry only a few steps behind. Instead of going down to his stomach, Henry grabbed the mic to his radio and took a knee.

Hunter could hear him whisper into the radio, but couldn't make out what was being said. A moment later he moved over to Hunter.

"You OK for POW search?" Henry asked in a low whisper.

Hunter nodded.

"Go back and meet Sergeant Frost and Corry at that generator," Henry continued.

Hunter nodded again, moved up to a knee and began to move back when Henry grabbed his arm. "You might need these," he said as he pulled two bars of C4 from his pant cargo pocket, handing them to Hunter. He reached into his other cargo pocket and handed over a coil of time fuse and a pliers-like crimping tool.

"You got the blasting caps," Hunter asked.

Henry nodded and pulled a small plastic container from his front breast pocket. Hunter put the materials into his own pockets, placing the caps that were inside the plastic case in his own front chest pocket.

Hunter stood and turned back toward the camp. He rapidly moved out of the bush, past the man he had just shot only minutes before, along the long building to the area where the tents were located. As he approached the area, he could see Sergeant Frost and Corry kneeling in front of the generator. When he reached their position, he went immediately to a knee.

"You two have to hurry the fuck up with this, but be thorough. We are kind of sitting out here with our ass in the wind. Don't miss anything; there could be some real important shit on some of these guys. And Hunter," Sergeant Frost looked up at him with a slight grin, "make sure the fucker is dead before you roll him."

Corry chuckled.

"Roger Sergeant," Hunter responded.

Both Hunter and Corry rose at the same time, moving toward the long building.

"Start where we came in?" Hunter asked.

Corry nodded, "Roger that."

The two went back down and over the small ravine they had encountered on the way in. On the other side they moved to the small sandbagged circle that the LBGs had been using for an LPOP.

Both individuals that had been in the hole were blown completely out of the small outpost and laid on the jungle floor, just outside. Both were facing up, neither had much for faces left. In fact, they both were completely riddled with holes and blood spots, one completely missing his arm.

"I don't think we have to worry about these bastards going for a grenade," Corry commented.

"Keep an eye down the trail; I'll search the first two," Hunter said as he kneeled in front of the first body."

"You sure man, I can start if you want."

"Na, I got it." Hunter first patted the man's two upper pockets, they were empty. He went to the two lower. There was something in it, as he pulled back the fabric to open the pocket the man's shirt separated revealing a mass of intestines. *Fuck, this bastard really got it,* he thought. Inside he found the man's cigarettes. *This was that dumb fucker that was smoking*. He patted down the pockets on the man's pants and found a bandana, some Panamanian money, and a pocket knife.

Hunter went to the second body and went through the same routine. This time he found several papers written in Spanish, and a small hand written map. He put these in his open cargo pocket. "Done, let's go. Grab that guy's weapon and ammo," Hunter whispered to Corry as he pointed to an AK-74 under the man's body." He grabbed the man's AK that he was working on, then took the magazines of ammunition he had on his web belt. He surveyed both bodies again to make sure they had everything.

Hunter could see Corry put his M-16 under his arm, as he lifted the man's body from the shoulder straps of his web belt. As he lifted, he grabbed the weapon and pulled it free. The weapon cleared its cover, the man's arm still attached, hanging from the trigger guard.

"Damn," Corry exclaimed. He dropped the man's body and the weapon to the ground. The arm landing a foot from the place it had once been attached. Corry stepped on the man's wrist and pulled the weapon free, handing it to Hunter. He bent over and crossed both men's legs, indicating that they had been searched.

Both headed back to the main compound, the search had only taken a few minutes. Once back at the long building, which Hunter dubbed "the shelter house", he put the two weapons on the long table with two others that where already there. Hunter could see Lancaster and Brady searching the bodies scattered in the main compound.

Hunter and Corry started on the west side, opposite of Brady and Lancaster, with the man that Hunter had hit before he got Henry, then continued with three others until they met up with the other team in the middle. Hunter found a regular map with several things written on it along with several papers written in Spanish, during the searches. The weapons that were collected were put in the shelter house in a large pile.

As Hunter placed a weapon on the pile from the last search, Sergeant Frost appeared to his side. "You got the demo to blow this shit?" he asked.

"Hooah Sergeant," Hunter replied.

"Blow that coke too," Sergeant Frost finished as he pointed to the cubes stacked on the end of the table. "Hurry up, we've already been here way too long. I want to be out of here in 5 mikes, got it?"

Hunter nodded, already reaching into his pocket for his ordinance. Working quickly, he retrieved all the explosive gear that he had received from Sergeant Henry and placed it on the table. Separating the coil of time fuse, he identified four different fuses, all cut at a length for three minutes. Hunter had personally timed and cut them when the platoon was prepping for the mission. The M-60 fuse igniters were already attached to the fuses. Hunter took out a blasting cap from the plastic holder, checked the well for debris, turned it upside down and shook it to ensure that it was unobstructed. He placed the cap on the time fuse, and then crimped it in place with his demo tool. He repeated the process for the other three pieces of time fuse.

On the two blocks of C4, Hunter made holes on both ends with the end of his demo tool for the blasting caps. *Double prime,* he thought as he worked feverishly. Once the holes were made, he pushed the caps deep inside the explosive, smashing the putty like substance around the time fuse that protruded. He did the same for the three remaining holes.

I'll blow it in two piles, Hunter thought. *I've got ten weapons and about twenty or so blocks of the coke, I'll just combine the piles.* He placed one block of C4 on the table and scurried to the other end carrying the other. He place the remaining block on the table beside the stack of drugs, and made a small platform with ten of the cubes of cocaine placing the C4 on top of them. Grabbing five of the remaining blocks, he went back to the end with the weapons and did the same. Once completed, he took five of the rifles to the other end and stacked them over the bed of coke and C4. He lifted the remaining five keys of coke, and repeated the process on the end that he had begun. As he finished, he took a split second to admire his work, *that'll do it* he thought.

Hunter went to the edge of the shelter house where he could see Sergeant Frost kneeling at the generator, as Corry and Lancaster were gathering what was left of the tents and their contents into a large pile. They had already cut all the guide ropes that were holding both tents up and were scooping the fabric into the middle. Judging from the large hump in the middle, they must had already put everything that was inside into the center. Hunter moved his hand up and down along the front of his body to get his attention.

Sergeant Frost shuffled over to the shelter house. "You ready to go?"

"Roger Sergeant."

"How much time do you have on the fuses?"

"Three minutes," Hunter responded.

"Alright," Sergeant Frost continued as he looked at his watch, "We'll get the squad on line about twenty-five meters on our next azimuth, I'll pop a thermite (Incendiary) grenade on each of the tent piles. When they go off, you pop the igniters."

"I'm going to need someone to help me Sergeant, I've got one on each end of the table and I want to pop them at the same time," Hunter interjected.

"OK," Sergeant Frost continued as he nodded. "We'll use Corry for rear security back here. I'll put both the thermites on the tents, then come back here and pull the other fuse igniter. We'll pull Corry just before, and all three of us will didi to the squads position. Got it?"

Hunter nodded.

Sergeant Frost grabbed the mic to his radio. "Red two, this is red one, over."

Sergeant Henry's voice came over the net. "Red one, this is red two, over."

"Red two, gather all red elements and move twenty-five meters on azimuth, over." Sergeant Frost looked over at Hunter as he released the send button on the mic. "Get Corry and bring him back, tell Lancaster to let Henry know that you two are with me, and we'll link up with them in about three mikes."

"Roger, out." Henry acknowledged his order that he had just been given over the radio.

Hunter scrambled back to the tent area where Lancaster and Corry were finishing. He grabbed Lancaster by the shoulder. "We're moving, link up with Sergeant Henry and let him know that Corry and I are going to pop the demo with Sergeant Frost. We'll link up with you in about three mikes."

Lancaster nodded and took off for the edge of the jungle where the rest of the squad was.

Corry came up on Hunter's left side and took a knee. Hunter immediately went down to his knee. "Your going to pull security while Sergeant Frost and I set off the demo."

Corry nodded.

Both men briskly walked back to the shelter house. As they approached, Hunter could hear Sergeant Frost on the net.

Sergeant Frost had his map out. "Roger, fire for effect to neutralize all remaining equipment on my command. I say again, on my command."

He's calling in Specter to blow the shit out of this place after we set off our demo. Good thinking, that will make sure there is absolutely nothing left here for them to use, Hunter thought.

Sergeant Frost pointed his fingers on the hand that was holding the map's edge toward his eyes, then pointed to the rear as he looked at Corry.

Corry immediately moved out several meters and went to the prone position, covering the area that Sergeant Frost had just pointed to.

"Lets get the fuck out of here," Sergeant Frost said as he put his map back into his side cargo pocket. "Get on the end and get ready."

Sergeant Frost ran over to where the tents were. Noticing that the generator was still between the two piles, he picked it up and set it next to the tent and debris pile to his left. He took out three thermite grenades and placed them on the ground next to him. Pulling the pin on the first one, he placed it directly in the center of the tent pile. The second grenade he rapidly placed on top of the generator. Grabbing the third grenade, he pulled the pin as he ran to the second tent pile and placed it in an indention on top, barely breaking stride as he continued to the shelter house.

Hunter had placed himself at the opposite end of the table where he had just talked to Sergeant Frost. He had grabbed both fuse igniters in his left hand, as he draped his weapon over his shoulder with the sling. With his right hand, he placed his index finger through both rings of the fuse igniters. He was ready to pull, and start the burning in the cord that would blow the charge in three minutes.

Looking up he saw Sergeant Frost come around the corner of the shelter house, and grasp his igniters in the same way that Hunter did. "Corry, Go," he shouted, not worrying about any noise at this point.

Corry ran past the shelter house in the direction the squad was moving out on.

"Pull in three," Hunter spoke, trying to control his excitement. "Three, TWO, ONE, PULL!"

Hunter looked down at the cord that protruded from each of the igniters. Both were smoking as they began to burn. 'BURNING!" he stated in an extenuated voice.

"BURNING!" Sergeant Frost remarked as he looked down at his fuse igniters.

Sergeant Frost and Hunter both moved at the same time, running toward the area of the jungle where the squad was suppose to be. As they entered the vegetation, both slowed to a brisk walk. A second later, Corry appeared. Looking forward, Hunter could see the rest of the squad.

Sergeant Frost rapidly moved his hand in a tomahawk motion, telling everyone to move out quickly.

The entire group rose from their positions and moved out quickly in a single file, five meters in-between each individual.

Damn what a rush, Hunter thought as he followed Corry.

The column moved another 50 meters before Sergeant Frost gave the signal to stop. Since Hunter was the last person in the movement he turned to face the rear. He glanced at his watch. *Should go off in about 30 seconds.*

As he waited, the jungle seemed especially quiet, except for the sound of his own heartbeat in his ears. In the distance, through intermittent holes in the canopy black smoke rising was rising height in the air, *the tents are on fire.* Hunter glanced at his watch again, only a few seconds left.

Hunter could hear Sergeant Frost on the Radio again, "Ghost Rider one nine this is red one over." There was a pause as they were answering the call.

The explosion shook the jungle. BOOOOOOOM. Echoing through the trees.

Sergeant Frost was back on the radio. "Roger Ghost rider one nine. Fire target. Target market with black smoke, how copy?" In the distance, the familiar droning hum of the Specter gunship engines came into ear shot. "Be advised, you have friendlies egressing 100 meters south of target." Sergeant Frost stood and gave the signal to move out again.

Everyone picked up and moved.

Hunter could hear the C-130 gunship getting closer. In front of Corry, he could hear Sergeant Frost still on the radio.

"Roger, I say again 100 meters south. All personnel north of target are enemy. I say again, all personnel north of target are enemy, you are clear to engage."

Damn, they must have been coming. Looks like we got out of there just in time, Hunter thought.

The same type of burping sound that he had heard the night he jumped in and pierced the sky. Hunter looked up to see the Gunship majestically sailing over his position, a stream of tracers were spewing from its side. *They are lighting them up with their mini gun.* Judging from the angle the tracers were on, they weren't too far from the camp.

The file of Rangers continued to move, intermittent expositions and bursts of mini-gun fire punctuating the trip. Soon they had traveled the distance back to friendly lines and the airfield. After a short stop, to call and let them know the squad was coming in, the line of individuals filed up the hill and through the lines in the same spot they had left the evening before.

CHAPTER 24

Emil waited long after the sounds from the airplane diminished from directly over the Lab.

He made his way to the trail that led up to the facility, shielding his eyes from the bright Sun that was radiating in through an opening in the canopy above. As he approached he could smell the death before he could see it.

There were two bodies at the guard post on the trail, both lying with their feet crossed. *Puntas!* Emil thought. *Desecrating the dead; I will make these Pigs die a slow painful death!*

He moved over into the main compound, finding many bodies in the same condition. There was still smoke rising from a scorched area where the tents had been, the fire looked to have burnt itself out only minutes before - the black smoke swirling lazily into the sky.

On the ground he found pieces of weapons scattered about, but nothing intact. As he made his way on the far side of the compound, he found several other bodies scattered about, these were different. Emil noticed immediately that they didn't have their legs and arms crossed like the others. He rushed over to examine his compadres.

The first soldier had a large gapping hole in his chest, beside him was his AK-74. Around his chest was a bandolier of ammunition. Emil pulled the bandolier of ammunition from the man's shoulder and placed it around his neck. He grabbed the AK-74 and ensured that the bolt moved freely and that there was a round in the chamber. *This will do*, he thought.

He headed north into the jungle. He would wait there until it was time to meet his compadres, they had something big planned. It would just be a few days before they could get together and launch it. For now he would be content to find a small village here in the hills and wait, thinking about the day when he could kill many more American pigs.

CHAPTER 25

Hunter was beat, his eyes burned with tiredness. As he sat down by his ruck, still in the same position around the tree, he noticed that he still had the ringing in his ears and that awful metallic taste in his mouth. Now that he thought about it, his nostrils were filled with the putrid stench of rotten meat and sweat. He grabbed his canteen and casually drank the entire thing.

As he looked around the perimeter, it seemed everyone was pretty much doing the same thing. For a split second, Hunter caught the sound of the Specter gun ship. He turned to see the C130 circling high over the jungle in the direction they had just came from. *They must still be mopping up*, he thought.

"Hunter." Henry exclaimed as he walked over to Hunter's position. "Get a new set of BDU's and your gear to get cleaned up. We're going to a swimming pool that's about 400 meters east of here, down the runway."

"Roger Sergeant," Hunter replied. *What a weird thing*, Hunter thought. *Taking a bath in a swimming pool essentially in the middle of the jungle.*

As Henry went back to his own ruck sack, Hunter dug into his. First he took out his extra waterproof bag that was neatly folded in one of the outside compartments of his pack. Spreading it out to fill it with the clothing that he was taking to change into, he noticed the holes. There were two bullet holes directly in the center of the bag. *That bastard ruined my bag*, remembering his initial exchange of gunfire after he had landed. Opening the waterproof bag inside the main compartment, he extracted a fresh set of BDUs, a new t-shirt, socks, and his shaving kit and placed them inside his not-so-waterproof bag.

When Hunter had finished getting his gear ready, he glanced around the circle of men in his squad. Lancaster and Henry were still getting inside their rucks, Donaldson from the M-60 squad was doing the same, but no one else was. *They're waiting for us to finish, so we can pull security for them,* he thought. Hunter went back down in the prone position to cover his side of the perimeter while the others got their gear out.

Several minutes later, Hunter looked around again to see everyone else rooting in their packs while the original group pulled security.

When everyone was ready, the squad moved out in three large wedge formations. Sergeant Henry's 1st team in front, Sergeant Singer's 2nd team in the rear, with Sergeant Frost and the M-60 team in the middle.

It was a short ten minute walk when the pool appeared in a cutout section of the jungle, between two small paste white buildings. Sergeant Singer's squad and the M-60 team pulled security while Henry's team went inside the fenced in pool to get cleaned up.

Hunter pulled off his gear and sat it next to fence, ten feet from the pools edge. The pool seemed remarkably clean; except for a few leaves floating in different places the water was crystal clear.

Sergeant Henry and Lancaster placed their gear next to Hunters.

"Looks refreshing, doesn't it?" Lancaster commented as he surveyed the area.

"Yeah, I'd say. I just can't wait to get this nasty shit off of me." Hunter said as he pointed to his neck and head.

Hunter took everything from his pockets and placed it on the concrete next to his ruck. He then took off his boots, placing them directly in front of his gear. Continuing until he was completely naked, he grabbed the saving kit from the top of his ruck, a fresh set of BDUs, and headed for the pool.

I'm definitely going to wash the nasty shit out of my uniform, he thought as he placed the wadded up bundle of clothing on the pools edge with his shaving kit. Hunter then walked to the end where there were steps leading into the shallow end. He quickly walked in, and completely immersed himself under the water.

"How's the water?" Henry asked as he removed the final remnants of his clothing.

"Nice and cool, feels like the pool back home in the middle of summer," Hunter replied.

"Don't get too relaxed, we've got to make this fairly quick so the rest of the squad can get in here. Hooah?"

"Roger Sergeant," Hunter answered. He walked to the edge and opened his shaving kit. Inside he grabbed the wash cloth and soap container that he had neatly packed several days ago. Hunter began to wash up. Once he had scrubbed his face, neck and upper body, he plunged under water to rinse. Wiping the water from his eyes, he could see a faint red ring circling his body, some of the reddish suds from the soap still floating on the surface.

The heavy chlorine in the water seemed to help the entire cleaning process, if only in his own mind.

Hunter finished the rest of his body standing on the steps, so he could clean his lower half. After finishing that, he walked back over to his bag proceeded to shave and wash his hair. *I feel so much better;* he thought as he grabbed his clothes and rinsed them in the water. He felt refreshed, if there was such a thing in a situation like this. It was still like a dream, real but not quite.

Once Hunter had finished cleaning his clothes, he placed them on the concrete on the edge of the pool and got out. Henry and Lancaster were just finishing up their own clothing. He walked over to his sopping pile of camouflaged material and rang each piece out, the water trickled off the side of the concrete toward the jungle.

"Hey, I'll put up some 550 cord at the corner of the fence so we can use it for a clothes line," Lancaster gestured to the opposite end of the pool area. "As hot as the sun is, I bet they'll be dry before the rest of the squad gets done."

"Hooah, sounds good." Hunter followed Lancaster down to the opposite end and attached one end of the parachute cord to the one side of the fence, while Lancaster attached the other. The line stretched across the corner of the pool about four feet off the ground.

Then it occurred to Hunter; this would look really ludicrous to someone looking at us. Naked guys taking a bath in a swimming pool and hanging out their laundry. He momentarily had to chuckle.

With the laundry done, and the bathing complete, the squad moved back to their original position and took turns sleeping. It was called 50% security, one person up on guard while the next slept. The sleep time was short, but effective. Hunter closed his eyes and instantly faded off. If he dreamed, he didn't remember when he was awakened an hour later. The whole thing still felt like a dream. *Maybe I'll really wake up and be in my bed back home in Ohio, back when things where easy, back when life and death weren't so intertwined.*

In the late afternoon the sound of the helicopters chop came into earshot. First starting as a very low distant hum, as if a truck was engine breaking down a distant hill, and then gradually growing into a loud slap as the CH-47 appeared over the tree tops. A second after the first came into view, an identical bird followed to the rear left, then another, and another. Moments later five of the large double rotered birds flew directly over the runway, majestically banked in a large loop and landed near the North edge of the runway clearing.

Hunter could feel the wind from the rotors, with the second aircraft only thirty meters from his position. As all five came to a rest on the ground, a flurry of troops poured from the rear of each bird dropping to their knees and stomachs as they cleared the exit ramp by ten meters or so. They formed a half circle around the Schnook.

"They're doing a combat exit," Hunter had to laugh. These guys were hitting the drop zone like it was hot, no doubt the future stories would stem from the epic battle where the 7th ID secured the airfield at Rio Hato, forgetting to mention the fact that Rangers had secured it a day and a half earlier. As the last troops exited, the lumbering giants picked up from the ground, one by one and swiftly disappeared in the direction they had came from.

Each of the five makeshift parameters began to move in different directions in large wedges, to predetermined locations. The platoon that had landed nearest Hunter's location made its way to the circle of Rangers stationed around the tree. The group stopped ten meters short with two individuals continuing on into 3rd Squad's area. After a brief halt for challenge and password, although it was a mute point in the daylight like this, they continued in to Sergeant Frost's location in the center.

As he glanced over his shoulder, Hunter could see that the person in the center talking to Sergeant Frost was a First Lieutenant from the 7th Infantry Division and his RTO (Radio Operator). Both knelt in front of Sergeant Frost, as he sat with his back against the tree eating some MRE crackers. Among a series of mumbles, Sergeant Frost pointed along the ridge where the rest of our platoon was stationed.

The Lieutenant nodded his head, rose to his feet and returned to his platoon. Soon the group was up and moving around either side of the structure. Several minutes later teams from the rest of the platoon started appearing, filling in spaces in the parameter. Within minutes Henry was tapping Hunter on the shoulder.

"Extend the perimeter out; make sure you and Lancaster have ten meters between you and the next two. We're going to be getting on a bird in about ten mikes," Henry reviewed in his normal methodical manner.

"Where to?" Hunter asked.

"Back to the airfield at Howard, we're going to prep for another mission there." Henry trotted off to the next two individuals in the circle.

Several minutes later the sound of a CH-47 again came into range. This time appearing from the inland edge of the airfield, flew straight for the Platoons position and landed twenty meters away. Two by two, the platoon stood and ran up the back ramp with rucksacks on back, weapons in hand, ten meters separating each pairing.

Hunter and Lancaster stood as Brady and Corry, on their right, began to run toward the waiting aircraft. They rapidly followed the string of individual under the rear blades and up the ramp. On the back ramp was a rear gunner, both hands firmly on the 50 cal that was posted in the center, each pair splitting on either side of the heavy machine gun.

Soon the platoon was aboard and rotary winged aircraft was rapidly moving skyward. Looking out the bubble like side windows of the helicopter, Hunter could see the ocean, the beach, the jungle. The smells of battle still fresh on his tongue, the sweet aroma that lingered within his nostrils and through everything that he tasted. The sick metallic taste of the blood, the taste that just wouldn't seem to go away. *I wonder who's blood it is? My own? Those little bastards? James's? I wasn't beside him when he met his destiny, but I should have been.*

As the two bladed aircraft rose swiftly from the field, the humming of the rotors seemed to drown out reality. The beach disappeared as the deep dark ocean seemed to engulf all that could be seen as the sun began to disappear beyond the horizon.

"Is this just a dream?" Hunter wondered. The constant buzz of the engine created an almost hypnotic atmosphere for all aboard. Soon several sets of eyes were closed, leaning on anyone or anything that was close enough for stability. Hunter could still hear one of his instructor's words from RIP, "Sleep when you get the chance, because you never know when you'll get another chance." Rangers often went days with very little or no sleep when on a mission, any short respite in a secure area was a welcome chance to recharge. Hunter's eyes slowly closed.

"HUNTER!"

Hunter looked quickly to his left. It was Lancaster.

"Damn it, GET US OUT OF HERE!"

The sky was dark, but constant flashes from artillery and illumination shells lit up the night like a strobe light. Between the flashes, the moonlight was good enough to see very well. They were in the rubble of a city. Bricks and blocks were scattered in piles all over the place. Hunter's whole squad was lined up against a half demolished wall.

Hunter looked down at his hands. They were bound together with wire ties.

"HUNTER, GET US THE FUCK OUT OF HERE!"

Hunter looked to his left again. Lancaster's face was dirty, covered with a combination of camouflage and dust. The panic in his eyes was explicit. His hands were bound as well.

High-pitched screams began to resonate through the debris. The kind of blood curdling screams that one expects from a child when they have really been hurt. But these weren't from a child, they were from a man. Between the screams, or between what seemed like the breaths that produced the screams, the distinct sound of laughter and conversation in Spanish could be heard. In the midst of it all a low humming that seemed to slow down and speed up with the breaks in the screams.

Hunter leaned forward to see the source of the screams on the opposite side of Lancaster. As another star cluster popped in the sky, the scene was illuminated. Three Hispanic men were holding an individual off the ground, one by the lower legs, one by the feet, and the other by the upper arms. The person they were holding was parallel to the ground, moving violently to get away, but they just looked too strong. The entire struggle seemed to be in vain. In front of the group, was a large band saw. The type of industrial equipment that one might find in a factory or large wood working shop Just beside the saw, were two large distinct piles, a two foot high and three foot across. One pile was hands, the other feet.

"HUNTER, DON'T LET THIS HAPPEN! YOU HAVE TO GET US OUT OF HERE!" The terror in his words radiated through Hunter. Ice ran down his spine. The horror was setting in, panic flowing through his veins, feeling as if inside a small room with the walls moving in. He pulled as hard as he could on the strips that bound his hands, the plastic cutting deep into his wrists.

Another bone chilling scream rang through the night. Hunter looked to the men maneuvering their victim so that the band saw was grinding through the man's hands; a dark stream of blood seemed to form a cloud around the blade. One hand fell to ground as the saw severed the last remnants of skin and bone.

"HUNTER!"

Hunter opened his eyes to see Corry from the corner of his eye. Hunter's eyes burned as the sweat beading on his face, running into his eyes. A gaping hole in his chest, and soul.

"HUNTER!" Corry shouted above the noise of the helicopter.

"YEAH, yeah," Hunter responded as he turned to look Corry full in the face.

"YOU ALRIGHT?" Corry's face showed genuine concern.

"YEAH MAN."

"DUDE, WE'RE ABOUT 30 SECONDS OUT – IT LOOKED LIKE YOU WERE STILL RACKING OUT WHEN THE COMMAND CAME THROUGH."

"YEAH, I WAS. . . THANKS," Hunter looked back out the side window to see that the aircraft was over land again, actually about a half a mile away from the ocean. Large numbers of houses began to appear along the coast.

The cold shiver that had run down his spine was still there, along with the gaping hole in his chest.

A truck was waiting on the ground as the Schnook landed on a taxiway at the Air Force Base. The platoon walked off the rear gate in two orderly lines, the Platoon Leader and the Platoon Sergeant leading the way to the truck.

The driver of the 2 ½ ton truck had the rear gate down and was posted to the side, ready to greet the incoming group. Both the Platoon Sergeant and the Platoon Leader stepped to the side as they approached, motioning into the truck. Each line successively loaded the truck from each side, first throwing their ruck sacks in, then pulling themselves up as they placed their foot on the foot-hold at the bottom of the gate. Soon the entire group was loaded, the rear gate closed, and the truck was in motion.

"Is this real?" Hunter mowed it over and over again in his head. "This just doesn't seem real. It's just like training." It just didn't seem right. He kept alternating between feeling like a hole was in his chest where his heart and soul was to absolutely nothing. No emotion at all, no feelings for anything. It just seemed like noting mattered anymore, except for his buddies. "I'll die before I let another one of my comrades go down."

The trip only lasted a few minutes. When the truck came to a halt, they were in front of a two-story structure that was obviously the post school. This would be their base of operations. The platoon unloaded and made their way to several different classrooms, each man picking up a cot from the rear of a cargo Hummer.

Third squad took a room on the first floor that was a second grade classroom. Paper cutouts of animals covered the walls; the entire gamut of wildlife seemed to be smiling. Along the top of the blackboard that covered the length of one wall, were large letters in cursive. All the desks were pushed against the back wall, each with name tags hanging from the front, only the front row was clearly visible.

What a contrast, Hunter thought, *an instrument of death housed in a bastion for the innocence of youth. You can see the joy of Heaven in children, I wonder if I will go to Heaven after this, I wonder if James is there? I know he is, I never knew a better man. It should have been me.*

The squad set up, and bedded down. They had a mission soon.

CHAPTER 26

They had drawn a prime mission; tonight would be one that they had trained for many times, hostage rescue. The platoon loaded back onto the duce-and-a-half that had transported them to the school earlier and moved back to the airfield.

The moon was full, almost 70% illumination. In the open field of the runway Hunter could see clearly all the different shapes of buildings and vegetation along the fenced in perimeter. The squad waited near one of the large hangers at the edge of the taxiway. They were in a cigar shaped perimeter watching and waiting. Hunter's stomach had the nervous butterflies of anticipation rattling around inside of him. . . as it always did on missions like this.

Soon the familiar buzzing of the aircraft came into earshot. Very low at first, but in a matter of seconds, each one of the helicopters landed just in front of their position. These were the MH-6, Task Force 160 special ops birds. They were like the ones from the first night in Rio Hato, except these had no mini-guns or rocket launchers on them, just benches on the outside skids. They were the equivalent to the small Hughes 500 commercial version, which just had enough room inside for the pilot and a passenger that sat directly beside him. Very small in terms of helicopters. Rangers used these aircraft for special missions to be inserted into a small specific spot quickly. On the outside of the aircraft, about two feet above the skids were two benches on either side to sit.

All four squad leaders, Sergeant Clinger, and Lt. Mahoney ran out to the lead aircraft to link up with the lead pilot. They huddled around the door opening, as they communicated. They had spoke to these same pilots several hours earlier in the mission brief they had attended here at the airfield. This was just the last minute link up to make sure nothing had changed. Third squad was on the third and fourth birds.

The group of leaders broke out from their huddle, almost as if they were in a football game, and ran back toward the platoon. Sergeant Frost signaled third squad to move forward. They would be on bird three. Sergeant Frost ran around the front of the third helicopter, ducking his head as he went. When on the other side, he waited for Hunter to reach him, and then pointed at the front spot. Hunter quickly grasped the hook on the end of his sling rope and hooked into the D ring at the mid section of the aircraft. Lancaster and Henry repeated the action directly behind him. The aircraft held a total of six Rangers, three on either side. When the other two were secured, they gave Hunter the thumbs up signal; he in turn looked over his shoulder to the pilot and repeated the gesture.

The aircraft lifted off the ground quickly and was soon zinging over the tops of the trees in the jungle, banking steeply now and then. The banking was so hard at times, Hunter's torso would be parallel with the ground. . . the G forces holding him securely in the seat. The ride lasted about ten to fifteen minutes when the pilot tapped Hunter on the shoulder. As Hunter looked, he gave him the 30-seconds signal with his hand. "Unhook!" Hunter struggled to reach behind his buddy and unhook his safety rope. Hunter unhooked his and handed it to him, then secured his own rope to his gear. His heart raced.

Hunter looked back at his team and gave the signal as he leaned toward them to voice the command. "Lock and Load." Hunter started beating his feet together; it always helped with the static electricity shocking his feet when they jumped off.

He pulled the charging handle of his SAW to the rear to chamber a round. Hunter could see the buildings of the town in front of the aircraft. They would be landing on the top of the three-story building toward the center of town, the main objective. The hostage was supposed to be in the south room of the 3rd floor. It was the team's job to neutralize any bad guys in the area, snatch the hostage and get him to an extraction bird as fast as possible.

The town was just on the other side of the canal, the lights of the city shimmering off the water as they rapidly approached. Hunter gripped his weapon tightly; he was very paranoid about dropping his SAW on the way into a firefight. *Kinda hard to fight with nothing to fight with*, he thought. Abreast of Hunter's aircraft there were several other MH-6 helicopters with different missions, basically to clear the rest of the area for Hunter's team to get the hostage. As they approached, Hunter identified their building. "Let's get some!" he thought. Hunter could clearly see the third floor and the top of the building.

He brought his SAW tight in his arm and pulled the trigger, strafing through the windows on the 3rd floors east sight until the aircraft was over the building, masking his fire. Hunter could hear his other team members doing the same between bursts of his own fire. The aircraft came to an abrupt halt as it hit the rigid surface of the flat roof. Everyone jumped off. A stinging pulse that felt like lightning shot through Hunter's legs, *it always seem to do that, no matter how hard you had beat your feet together.* Hunter hit the ground, and the bird was off.

Hunter and Brady immediately ran to the east side of the building, pulling out their home made special concussion grenades (grenades that explode with blinding light and noise, but have no deadly shratenal) while the rest pulled security. They had taken about ten feet of 550 cord and attached them to the devices so we could toss them out and make them swing back into the windows. Both activated the grenades at the same time, and swung them out over the edge. Both grenades entered the windows. Both men letting go of the cord so that they would drop into the room.

"They're in," Hunter yelled.

Henry and Lancaster came over to the edge and knelt down with the special ladders. The ladders which tri-folded, were carried in the small rear cargo section of the aircraft. While Hunter and Brady were dropping the concussion grenades in, Henry and Lancaster had extended one section completely, and the other so it made an upside down V to hook over the edge.

Boom, Boom. The grenades went off one after another. Henry went over the edge first, and popped into the window as Hunter slung his weapon and looked over the side. After he had entered, Hunter eased over the edge and down the ladder to the opening of the window. Henry reached for his hand and pulled him in. The room was extremely dark; Hunter lunged forward to the nearest wall and knelt. He scanned the area for any movement. None. Hunter turned on his flashlight attached to the forearm assembly of his SAW. He scanned the area again with the beam of light as the next person was coming through the window. There was no one in the room. "CLEAR," He yelled. As each member of the squad entered the room they went to a wall and covered an area of the room.

To Hunter's front was the door to the south room where the hostage was, or at least where Intel had said the hostage was being held. Hunter kept his weapon trained on the door. As two from the other team cleared the room to his rear, Hunter watched the door. "CLEAR'" rang out from one of the team members. "They must all be in that room," He thought. Lancaster came up on the other side of the door and checked the handle.

It was open. *"Low and left, low and left,"* Hunter thought. *"ID targets, ID targets, there's a good guy in there."* Hunter was going in first.

Lancaster nodded. Hunter stood up and kicked the door as hard as he could with his left foot and lunged forward into the room with his SAW on his shoulder sighting down the barrel. As he entered he heard movement to his left. It was a large room. Hunter pivoted, moving left, the beam of his flashlight illuminating a camouflage clad individual with an assault rifle. There was a short three round burst from behind him as Lancaster was engaging other targets in the room. Hunter held the trigger of his weapon for a six round burst. The rounds hit center mass of the individual, splintering the stock of his AK-47 assault rifle and impacting in the man's sternum. The burst threw the enemy soldier rearward, he seemed to fly to the rear momentarily, with his toes dragging the ground. As Hunter crouched, he quickly swung the beam of light from the front of his machine gun to the left target in time to be momentary blinded from the muzzle flash. He pulled the trigger as the deafening cracks filled the room. Hunter's weapon unloaded a long burst of thirty rounds. As Hunter desperately tried to adjust his eyes he searched the area for movement from the other man in the room. As the area came back into focus, he could see the pile of the man who had engaged him.

"CLEAR," Lancaster yelled.

Hunter rapidly scanned the rest of his side of the room. "CLEAR." He could see the light from Lancaster's weapon moving rapidly over his side of the room.

"I've got one enemy down!" Lancaster stated.

"I got two" Hunter repeated in a monotone statement.

"Anybody hit," Sergeant Henry asked as he entered the room cautiously.

"I'm good," Lancaster shot back.

"Good," Hunter stated, as he continued probing the room.

"You got the hostage," Sergeant Frost yelled from the adjacent room. Hunter rapidly scanned the room from end to end once again. There was no one else there. "He's not here!"

"ARE YOU SURE?" he exclaimed

Just then Lancaster and Hunter simultaneously noticed a large box in the middle of the room. "The box!" both said in unison. It was a three-foot by three-foot square with large holes drilled in the top, encircled by razor wire. "Wait One." Hunter responded

Lancaster went to the wire, "Anybody in there?" There was no response.

After examining it for booby traps, he used his wire cutters that had hung around his neck to snip through the wire. "Anybody in there?" he repeated.

This time there was a faint moan.

"He's in a box!" Hunter yelled back to Sergeant Frost. "We need a crow bar."

Brady came running in with a crow bar, and gave it to Lancaster. He pried the top, which had been nailed shut, open; he was there.

Meanwhile Hunter covered the corner of the room where the stairwell led down to the next floor. The rest of the squad entered the room. Hunter moved up to the edge of the stairwell. He could hear his squad leader calling on the radio. "Roger Bravo two five, we have precious cargo. Repeat - we have precious cargo. Over."

Henry came up behind Hunter and pulled out a grenade. "Alright, let's go."

He pulled the pin and threw it down the steps. Boooom, the building shook and dust flew from the ceiling with the explosion. Hunter leaped to the outside wall of the stairs and moved quickly down them hugging the wall to see as far down as he could, his team leader just on his rear. Both scanned the second floor room as they approached. "CLEAR," Hunter yelled. Henry continued past Hunter's rear and down to the first floor. Hunter following close. Henry fired as he traversed the final steps to the ground floor. As Hunter's view became open he could see a figure falling to the floor. A second later Henry yelled "CLEAR!"

The rest of the squad was close behind and scooted down the stairs behind Hunter and Henry. One door separated the small stairwell room from the street outside. Hunter quickly glanced over his shoulder to see Brady and Lancaster carrying the hostage from either side of the battered individual. This was the first opportunity that Hunter had to see him. He was very skinny, with tattered clothing; his face covered with a combination of dirt and dried blood. He looked to be in his 50's, and under different circumstances cleaned up could be construed as a businessman.

Hunter could hear Sergeant Frost on the radio again, "Bravo two five this is Bravo three eight, Ready to move to extraction. Over."

After a short pause while he listened, Sergeant Frost responded, "Roger."

"Go, Go, Go" Sergeant Friar said as he got to the first floor.

As the last member of his squad moved behind him, he yelled Hunter's name, signaling that he was the last, while Hunter covered their movement. Hunter picked up and followed out the stairwell, watching over his shoulder as he went. The squad ran across the street toward an alley that led into what appeared to be an open lot. As he followed, he could hear the rotors of the HH-53 Jolly Green Giant helicopter coming in. Brady and Lancaster were now dragging the hostage between them with each of his arms over their shoulders. Hunter glanced over his shoulder to check the rear, as he did every few steps.

As they ran down the alley, he could see the corridor set up in an open area just on the other side of the buildings. There were Rangers on both sides a few feet apart on either side forming the edges of a little road into the opening. As the squad cleared the buildings and ran down the corridor, the aircraft was landing with its rear gate down. Everyone ran up the ramp into the rear of the aircraft. As soon as Hunter was in, the bird took off.

Hunter looked at his watch. The entire thing had taken nine minutes.

It was a short trip to the airfield where a group of men in colored shirts were waiting on the tarmac. As the helicopter landed, they ran up the ramp and grabbed the man who was sitting in one of the crew seats along the side of the aircraft. No words were said; they assisted him off the ramp and into a hanger. The 53 lifted off, and swept into the darkness. Several minutes later the group was landing back at the airstrip Howard Air Force Base where they had started the mission less than an hour before.

When the adrenalin stopped flowing, it was almost as if the on switch had been turned off. Hunter's entire being felt exhausted. Soon they were back at the school, in the dainty classroom. He could almost feel the wave of joy that the room seemed to exude as he entered; a joy that childhood is filled with. The joy of Christmas, the joy of a crush, the joy of playing. With a breeze that flowed into the room like a silent wrath, the smell of the jungle brought back the reality of death. The reality of emptiness that now seemed to be everywhere.

The squad cleaned their weapons and gear, everyone seemed to be in a daze. It seemed the long hours with very little sleep were starting to wear on everyone. As one person would finish, they would help others in the squad. Soon they were all clean.

"Hit the rack," Sergeant Frost announced. "First platoon's pulling security for the rest of the night."

Hunter moved his ruck from the cot and pulled the poncho liner from inside. He placed his weapon next to the area his head would occupy, arranging his web belt with his combat knife on top with in an arms reach, "just in case." Removing his BDU top, he rolled it into a makeshift pillow and placed it at the end of his bed. He pulled the blanket like liner over his body, even though it was still 80 degrees, and rolled onto his side.

"HUNTER!"

Hunter shot up in his cot, instantly grasping the knife that was next to his portable bunk. His left hand reaching out to grab an invisible enemy. His eyes tried to focus in the dark, his brain not making sense of the dramatic change of environments. The sweat poured from his brow, the front of his t-shirt soaked. His eyes search for an enemy, they were gone.

It's a dream. It's a dream. Hunter lay back down.

CHAPTER 27

It was Christmas morning, but it sure didn't feel like it to Hunter. It was 5:00 AM and it was already getting hot. The school that they were staying at was comfortable enough, they even had cots. As Hunter prepared his gear for the mission, he had only one Christmas wish. "Please God; don't let me die on Christmas Day." Hunter knew if he got killed today, it would ruin the holiday for his family forever.

Hunter's platoon went to the airfield and boarded their helicopters. Hunter's platoon was all on an HH-53, Jolly Green Giant. They sat in rows along the length of the aircraft on the floor. On the rear tailgate was a crewmember with a 50 caliber machine gun, and on the two front side doors there were mini-guns. Hunter was sitting at the rear of the aircraft with two people between him and the tailgate on the right side, next to the window. Today's mission was an airfield seizure. But it wasn't to be the kind they usually did. Instead of parachuting in at night and clearing the runway, they were getting inserted by helicopter and were just to secure the perimeter. Hunter's platoon was to take out the terminal and the southern gate.

As they flew over the sea, Hunter began to check his gear and relax when the mini-guns opened up. Then the 50 caliber machine gun just to his front right began to clamor over the noise of the aircraft. Hunter instinctively grabbed for his SAW. As he looked out the rear he confirmed that they were still over the sea, "what the fuck is going on?"

The firing stopped after just a second, and the gunner looked up. Test firing. They were test firing their weapons before going into a hot LZ (Landing Zone).

The rest of the ride was uneventful. Hunter watched as the blue landscape of water out the back of the helicopter turned to green when they made it back over land. Soon the whining pitch of the rotors changed their tone and an unmistakable feeling of slowing ran through Hunter's body.

The gunner on the rear of the aircraft put his hand to his ear that was covered by his headphones and looked out over the plush green countryside as he listened. He then turned back to the group. "Six minutes . . . Stand UP"

The squatting mass of green began to lumber up in an undulating wave. The individuals on the outer edges who could find hand holds on the aircraft stood first with the others in the group pushing them to their feet. Soon the entire group was standing, each man holding onto their weapon with one hand and their buddies with the other.

Hunter, standing near the tail gate, leaned back to the rear so that a sudden lurch from the aircraft would not throw him over the edge. "What a way to die," he thought. "Dear Mr. and Mrs. Hunter, your son died because he was stupid and fell out of a helicopter." It certainly would not bode well for the memory of PFC Jim Hunter.

The gunner turned back to the group again, "Thirty seconds. . . Lock and Load!"

Here we go, it's go time! Hunter pulled back the charging handle of his SAW to chamber a round, and then released the slide forward as a 5.56 round slide into the chamber. He glanced over his left shoulder toward the circular window in the side of the aircraft. Outside he could clearly make out a group of people; it looked to be 100 to 150 personnel on the LZ. The helicopter was still 50 feet in the air and rapidly descending.

Oh my God they are waiting for us and were coming in here in broad daylight. Hunter looked at his weapon. *I don't have enough bullets to kill all of those people!* A lump began to grow in his throat.

The aircraft rapidly descended the remaining 50 feet. Hunter flexed his knees to absorb the impact that he knew was coming from the speed of the helicopters movement toward the ground.

The Jolly Green Giant impacted the ground hard, had the Rangers not been packed in so tight many would have surely fell. The Gunner screamed over the rotor wash, "GO, GO, GO!" Swinging his left hand in a swimming motion to indicate it was time to get off the bird.

Hunter sprinted to the right side of the aircraft, just as he had been trained, and ran ten steps toward the mass of people – fully expecting to take a few rounds in the chest. He then planted his knees in the ground, put the butt stock of his weapon in the ground and fell forward into a prone fighting position, directly behind his weapon. Sighting directly down the barrel of his SAW he could clearly make out the group of people just 50 meters away. His right hand clicked off the safe button. He could clearly make out faces, they were dressed in street clothes, there were women, and children. They seemed to be . . . clapping? They were clapping, all of them.

The helicopter took off and moved quickly over the tree line at the far end of the airfield. The loud noise of the rotor blades faded. As the sound faded, another took its place. Cheering? It was cheering and clapping, Hunter could clearly distinguish the sounds now. What the Hell?

Hunter used his thumb to put his weapon back on safe. The clapping and cheers continued for another minute.

Sergeant Frost came up and knelt next to Hunter, "S2 told the guys that held this airfield we were coming, apparently the word got around town. We need to make our way to the terminal and secure it. Be ready to move as soon as I brief the rest of the Squad." He moved to Henry's position to relay the same information.

A few minutes later, Sergeant Frost had briefed everyone and he stood and motioned with his hand toward the large structure directly on the other side of the still cheering crowd.

Hunter stood and began to walk toward the crowd. As he approached the crowd, they parted to let him through. Several people slapped him on the shoulders.

"We love you!" a girl shouted from his right. "America number one!" another man yelled with a thick Spanish accent. It seemed they all wanted to touch him. The group would part as he moved forward and fill in all around him as he passed. A little girl walked up to him and tried to hand him a bottle of Coke. Hunter shook his camouflaged head and face and smiled through the light green and lomb face paint at the little girl.

Soon the squad emerged from the mass of people in front of the terminal building. They entered and systematically cleared each room with no resistance. Sergeant Frost keyed his radio and spoke into the mike, "Red One, this is Red Three, we're clear. Over." There was a long pause, then he responded again "Roger, Out."

"We need to move to the far North end of the airfield. There is a cement building that needs to be cleared. We're going to set up there for the night."

The squad all picked up and began moving toward the building.

It was exactly what they had said, a twenty feet by twenty feet cinder block building. It took the squad ten minutes to cover the ground between the Terminal and the block building. When they arrived they found a single metal door on the opposite side of the structure. Some prying with a crow bar that Lancaster had brought opened the door fairly easily.

The Squad moved through the two rooms of the structure quickly, clearing it in the same manner they had cleared the Terminal. The rooms were for some sort of administrative function, as both were filled with filing cabinets and a desk each.

After securing the building, the squad spread out in a large circle around the structure. This would be their Patrol Base for the night. Ten minutes later Henry came over to Hunter's position. "How's it going?" he asked.

"Great Sergeant" Hunter responded.

"Do you need anything?"

"No Sergeant. What do you make of this building?" Hunter gestured toward the cinder block building as he looked it over. The blocks were faded to a dirty white gray color, the roof was flat, with electrical and telephone wires coming into the corner.

"I don't know, some type of administrative building or something" Henry followed Hunters gaze over the building. "They have power and telephone."

Hunter and Henry looked at each other, a broad smile emerging on both men's faces. They said in unison "telephone!"

It had been two weeks since Hunter had called his family at home. When they were alerted for the mission everything was locked down. No communication with the outside world. All they knew was that Hunter was supposed to be home on leave and he just never showed up. He was sure they would have put two and two together when they heard about the invasion, but he knew his mother had to be worried sick.

"Let me see if the phones work, I'll be right back." Henry quickly moved back in the building. Several minutes later he emerged, smiling from ear to ear. He nodded toward Hunter, and made his way over to Sergeant Frost. A minute later he was back at Hunter's position. "I just cleared it with Sergeant Frost, we're gonna call home. I'll go first, when I'm done I'll take your position and you can call. We will take turns all around the perimeter so everyone gets a chance. Got it?"

Hunter nodded with a smile, "Roger that."

Henry was in the structure for fifteen minutes and then came over to Hunter's position. "You're up"

Hunter stood and walked into the building. He went to the first office to the left. There was a phone directly in the middle of the desk. He picked up the receiver and dialed zero.

A women's voice answered in Spanish, Hunter couldn't understand what she said.

"Do you speak English?" Hunter asked.

"Yes."

"I need to make a collect call to the United States?"

"Please hold. . . what's the number you are calling"

Hunter gave her his parent's phone number. The phone began to ring. No answer. That's right, they would be over to his Grandpa and Grandma's house for Christmas morning.

The operator came back on the line, "I'm sorry there is no answer at that number."

"Could you please try one more number?"

"Yes."

Hunter gave her his grandparent's phone number. This time his Grandpa answered.

"Hello"

"Hi Grandpa, its Jim. Is my Mom there?"

"You OK?"

Hunter pause a moment. *Could anyone ever really be ok after something like this? What was ok, was it that he was physically still intact, or was it that he would never be the same again. Never look at things the same way, never be able to relate to the people back in the real world? How could he ever make someone understand the things that he had seen, if they hadn't been there themselves?*

"Yeah, I'm good. Tell everyone not to worry."

"Hold on, I'll get your mom."

A few seconds later Hunter's mother's voice came on the line, "Jim?"

"Yeah mom, it's me."

She immediately broke down in hysterical tears.

"It's ok mom, I'm ok. I can't tell you where I'm at, but I'm ok." Normally tears from his mother would elicit a response in Hunter, this time it didn't. All he felt was emptiness.

Overwhelmed with emotion, she handed the phone over to Hunter's dad.

"Hey pal! How's it going?"

"I'm good," Hunter responded. How could he compact everything that had happened into a five minute phone call, even if he wanted to. Which he didn't, there was no way his father could understand. It was good just to let them know that he was alright. "I really can't talk; I just wanted to let you know I was ok."

"How long will you be gone? We've been watching the news."

"I'm not sure; I'll call you as soon as I can."

"Ok, you be careful."

"I will, I'll talk to you soon. Good bye."

"Bye."

Hunter hung up the phone and made his way back to his position. *It will never be the same. I don't even know if I could go back to the real world and fit in. There was so much I wanted to do in this life, so much I wanted to accomplish. Now it really might be better if I don't make it home from this.*

CHAPTER 28

The entire platoon sat in a small room with small fogged windows that stretched along the top of the outer walls. The brilliant sunlight from outside disbursed through the windows to fill the room with a glow that almost hurt the eyes.

There was a large map of the area tapped to the wall, another makeshift written map made with four 8 ½ X 11 sheets that were tapped to top corner of the larger one. The platoon's mission would be to raid a known PDF strong hold and gather as much information as possible on the group's members, activities, and plan for repelling the invasion.

"Intel says that the house at this intersection," the Lieutenant pointed to a section of the map, "has important information on a major counter attack that the PDF is planning in the near future. Our mission is to clear the house and gather all intelligence located within so we can stop the attack. Any questions?"

All the camouflage faces in the room shook their heads simultaneously.

CHAPTER 29

The Blackhawk lifted off quickly, very quickly, Hunter could feel what seemed to be three times his entire body weight smashing him to the floor of the aircraft. Hunter liked the thrills of rollercoaster, parachuting, fast roping, and the nap of the earth flying they had done in the past, but this seemed to be more - more that any rollercoaster or jump he had ever had. It was a precursor of the flight to come.

Hunter pulled his SAW tight to his body. *If I lose this I'm dead.* The aircraft continued to accelerate up and forward. The wind blowing through the open doors on the sides of the helicopter was like a hurricane.

Hunter reached down to check his connection to the floor of the aircraft. He had his sling rope tied securely around his waist, a two foot lead with a snap link on the end that was his umbilical to the rings on the floor of the Black Hawk.

Suddenly the bird banked hard left, bringing the shadowy ground fully into view with the entire aircraft completely sideways. Hunter could feel the centrifugal forces pulling his body tight into the floor. He had to tense all his muscles to keep his entire body from collapsing. Instantaneously, the bird righted itself again, dropped down, leaving Hunters stomach in his throat. *This is nap of the earth!*, Hunter could feel an uncontrollable grin erupt on his face.

The Black Hawk went through a series of turns and twists as it raced just feet above the treetops. Several times Hunter thought he saw the rotor blades hit the tops of trees as they maneuvered.

Hunter looked up to see the pilots in the front of the aircraft. Directly behind each pilots seat was the door gunners. Each had both hands firmly on the handles of their mini-guns that protruded from each side of the bird. In the center of the two gunners was the crew chief.

The crew chief looked back and forth between the front and the squad tied to the floor in the rear. "THIRTY SECONDS!" The crew chief held on tightly with his right hand and presented the signal with his left. Hunter could feel the adrenalin surge through his veins again. All the hair on his entire body stood on end. He reached over and broke the chem-light on the end of the rope, making it glow, then quickly traced his sling rope with his hand down to the snap link where it connected to the floor. The chem-light would allow him to tell when the end of the rope was on the ground. *Get ready, Get ready.* Hunter could see a red glow getting brighter out the right side door as the trees flew by. He grasped the charging handle of his SAW, pulled it forcefully to the rear and released it to chamber a round.

The aircraft made an extremely violent right turn; Hunter could feel the nose of the helicopter pull skyward, banking hard to reduce speed quickly. It was the procedure for every fast rope: in hard and fast, nose up to stop, kick the ropes and go!

The crew chief's head snapped to look at the Rangers in the rear, as he turned his face contorted in an intense grimace. He began to scream over the hum of the aircraft. "WE'RE GOING IN HOT!" Just as he finished the last syllable, the mini-guns opened up on both sides, the flashes of light dancing through the dark silhouettes in the cabin. The noise was deafening, like a massive hive of giant bees. Hunter released his snap link from its secured position on the floor and stuffed it and the tail of the rope into his cargo pocket.

This is it, this is it baby. It all went into automatic. It always seemed to for Hunter, it extended past the training. He seemed to get into the same "zone" in pressure situations, whether it was sports or training. The massive influx of endorphins in his system must have some type of overriding auto piloting effect.

"GO, GO, GO," the Crew Chief motioned with both hands in a tomahawk motion toward each door as he tried to scream above the noise.

Hunter kicked the coiled rope out the door opening with his right foot, as his stomach drove further up his throat. *I'M GONNA DIE, I'M GONNA DIE.* He grabbed the rope just outside the door, two feet down from its connecting point on the aircraft. Staring downward, he could see the chem-lights stationary glow on the dark surface of the ground. *ITS ON, IT'S ON THE GROUND!*

Hunter leapt from the aircraft, sliding down the rope like a fire pole. As he slid, he could see the village clearly, the entire scene was illuminated by two cars burning in the street. He used his gloved hands only to guide his fall and break slightly as he impacted the ground. Using the same parachute landing fall from jump school he rolled away from the end of the rope, leaping up into a full sprint toward the nearest building.

A stream of tracers from one of the mini-guns was pummeling into the second story windows as Hunter reached the ground floor. It almost seemed like a laser beam cutting into the structure, debris rained down as the bullets ripped apart the wood and glass.

The string of warriors flew out the sides of the helicopter and flowed down the two ropes suspended on each side. Each rope suspended with soldiers one on top of each other until they hit the ground and rolled to one side or the other. When all had exited the aircraft, the ropes were released and the Blackhawk wisped away over the trees.

The entire squad rushed up only seconds behind Hunter, lining up against the wall.

"Go, Go," Henry whispered as the last people out of the Blackhawk moved in behind.

Hunter moved along the wall until he came to the first window. He ducked underneath, so anyone inside could not see him, and continued to the edge of the structure. Each successive man in the line ducked under the window in the same way. Each individual in the "stack" of men covered a different area as they moved. The front individuals covered in the direction of movement while the rear people covered the back and the top of the buildings.

When he reached the edge, Hunter quickly peeked around the corner. He could clearly see the car burning in the street, there were no other figures were visible. There was a small alcove just around the corner – presumably with a door in it leading inside the building they were against.

Their mission during this operation was relatively simple, clear out the building they were now outside, recover any PIR (Priority Information Requirements) and get it to S1(Intelligence). The key was going to be getting the information before the people inside had a chance to destroy it. If they knew they were going to be overrun they would raze all paperwork immediately. Hopefully the fireworks from the Apaches on the cars and the raking of the building by the mini-guns had distracted them enough that they hadn't had a chance to get rid of anything.

Hunter glanced over his left shoulder, "I've got an alcove with a closed door around the corner."

Henry responded instantly, "I'll kick, you clear with Corry." He then turned to relay the information over his shoulder to Corry.

"Ready?" Hunter asked.

"Ready!" Henry said in an excited voice.

Hunter swiftly flew around the corner with Henry on his shoulder. As they rounded the structure Hunter stepped to the left and pointed his SAW directly at the closed door. Henry stepped forward and kicked the door with his right foot. The door flew open as Henry stepped away to let Hunter and Corry through.

Hunter exploded through the door. *Low and left, low and left.* As he entered the room he identified two targets. Both seemed to have been looking out the front windows of the building, AK-74s raised, apparently preparing to fire out at something outside. They were both startled by the sudden interruption into the room and were spinning to point their rifles at Hunter.

Hunter immediately tracked on the motion and brought this SAW to bear on the two men who where standing in line from where Hunter entered the room. He pulled the trigger hard. BUZZZZZZZZZZZZZIT. The rounds impacted both figures center mass, throwing them rearward.

As Hunter engaged the two targets at the front windows, a third enemy soldier entered through the door at the right rear of the room. Hunter saw the figure milliseconds after letting his finger off the trigger, but it was too late. The soldier had his AK raised pointing directly at Hunter. Two loud shots rang out in the room. Hunter waited for the pain, waited for the burning, waited for the end.

Instead the soldier convulsed as two bullets impacted his chest. Hunter looked back to see Corry with his weapon leveled at the man.

"CLEAR!" Corry shouted.

Hunter paused a minute, then yelled "CLEAR!"

The room was desolate save for a single table in the center of the room with a single light bulb hanging over it. The table was full of papers and maps.

"I've got Intel," Hunter exclaimed. Corry went back to cover the open door leading to another room.

The lieutenant entered the room a moment later with his interpreter in tow. They poured over the paperwork for a moment, speaking to each other in hushed tones while Hunter checked the bodies.

"This is it," the lieutenant said to the squad, "Let's get out of here."

CHAPTER 30

The sun set in the Western sky, it seemed to burn into the horizon.

Will this be my last time? Hunter thought. It really didn't seem to matter that much. Not like before. It was like he still had that strong instinct to survive, but it had diminished. It just wasn't quite the same. That dull ache that permeated his soul was still there. But there was more of a void.

The duce and a half (2 ½ ton truck) pulled up on the street adjacent to the patrol base.

"Our limo is here," Sergeant Frost noted in a monotone sneer.

The two and a half ton truck glided to a stop, its breaks squealing loudly. The headlights blazed like laser beams spotlighting the building to its front.

It had got dark very quickly, real dark. The overcast sky seemed to block any remnants of light. Zero illumination.

It was a little unnerving, complete darkness. Hunter had a flashlight attached to the forearm assembly of his SAW, but that was strictly for room clearing. He liked the dark, a little bit of natural cover that could hide you from the enemy. The problem came into play in identifying targets with no illumination - especially inside buildings. The beams of faded light that would inevitably stream in through windows were always good to light up a room with a kaleidoscope of black and white silhouettes. To effectively identify targets they used the flashlights attached to their weapons. It seemed to Hunter that that method still left a little to be desired. You could only see the circle directly in front of your weapon, not the rest of the room. It was great for scanning the room directly, terrible for peripheral vision. The flashlight also had a couple of bad consequences of use; it killed your night vision in your shooting eye outside the beam of light and it acted like a laser beam showing anyone who could see the light exactly where you were.

"Time to load", Sergeant Frost whispered to the squad.

Hunter rose from his position, instinctively checked to make sure his weapon was on safe, and shuffled in the file of Rangers moving toward the truck. He reached out and grabbed the dark silhouette in front of him, "Who is this?"

"Lancaster", a voice whispered back. Good, he knew who was in front of him. It was standard practice, making sure you were following the right person. Sometimes when the whole platoon got up and moved in the night, just like now, you could get out of place when it was really dark. Not only was it an orientation thing to find out where you where in the group, but it was for safety as well. A bad guy could step into a formation in the dark night and follow along to find out where the group was going. Wait for the right time and drop a grenade into the patrol base.

Hunter felt a tug on his shoulder.

"Who is this?" Brady's suppressed voice whispered.

"Hunter"

"Roger that. Man it's fucking dark tonight." Brady continued to walk toward the truck.

As the file of men reached the rear of the duce and a half, they bunched again as they waited when the people in front of them loaded onto the truck.

The truck was being loaded from both sides of the rear. The trucks bed was at chest level. When the gate was opened and swung down it formed a foot hold on either side to assist in personnel loading. Now each individual slung his weapon over his back, to free up both hands, and waited to climb up into the deuce and a half.

Hunter waited in the group. Several people loaded. Then it was his turn.

He put his foot in the slot on the left side of the vehicle. A hand shot out of the inky darkness to lift him up. He grabbed the hand with his right and pulled hard. He sprung up into the complete darkness of the covered bed of the truck. He un-slung his weapon and felt his way to the bench seat on the side of the bed.

When Hunter felt a knee, he spun his butt around and sat on the seat next to it.

"Pack it in, pack it in tight. We've got to get the whole platoon on this deuce!" Sergeant Clinger's harsh voice carried through the back of the truck.

Hunter pushed sideways on the seat toward the front of the vehicle to make sure there was no space between him and the next person. A second later, the person on his right was doing the same. He could make out the half moon opening at the rear top of the truck. It appeared that the truck was almost completely loaded.

There was a "clank" of metal on metal as the rear gate was closed. Then a banging of chain on metal as the small chain that held the gate retaining pins were inserted to hold the gate closed. The silence cut through the inky night.

Hunter reached over to his left, "Who is this?"

"Brady"

He reached to his right, "Who is this?"

"Slovack" A very thickly accented Spanish voice replied.

A million things when through Hunter's mind instantly. Who *the hell was Slovack? Was it like one of those stories that they were taught so many times, where a bad guy sneaks into the formation at night. His knife was on his LBE which was packed between him and Slovack, no way to get at it quickly. His SAW was wedged between his legs in the mass of humanity with the barrel facing the floor. He was going to have to go hand to hand.* He raised his left hand to deliver the first blow to the face.

"Slovack who?!" the words came out as a hiss.

Hunter's fist tightened. He could just make out the dark mass that was his head. The first blow would be enough to incapacitate. He would then go for the throat. A chill ran through his back as the adrenaline began to course through his veins.

"HUNTER!" an alarmed voice came from the floor. "HE'S THE SF INTERPRETER" It was Sergeant Frost.

The words came, but in a dreamlike state.

"HUNTER!" Sergeant Frost's voice came a little louder this time.

"SSS Sergeant?"

"He's the interpreter."

The words rang home. This was the interpreter in case we needed to interrogate any PDF on the mission. *I almost killed our interpreter! That would not have been good.*

Hunter's body unwound instantly. He lowered his hand.

The rest of the ride was uneventful. Twenty minutes later the truck came to a stop with the high pitch scream of the breaks.

Hunter's heart began to race again. *Thump – thump, thump – thump.* He could feel it in his veins and hear it in his ears.

The back flap of the trucks canopy flopped open.

"Let's get off this deuce and a half!" Hunter thought *"those breaks had to have woken up the whole neighborhood!"*

The group quickly poured off the truck into the street. Hunter jumped from bed of the truck and stumbled slightly before regaining his composure.

He moved forward to let the others behind him get off, then made a quick right to link up with his squad on the driver's side of the vehicle.

Intel had said that this place in David was an extreme hot bed of activity. In their mission brief they had reviewed how this weapon's cache was laid out, the number of guards, and the way they were going to infiltrate and seize the weapons. The problem was, there may be a lot more than the four PDF guarding the weapons that Intel had sited. If the word had got out about the invasion, and the word had definitely got out by now, there could be a whole platoon of them in there.

The street was deserted. The houses were made with stucco that even with the dirty exterior, seemed to glow slightly in the very dim light. The house they were concerned with was at an intersection about a block away from where they were dropped off. The plan was to quickly traverse the small alleys, doorways and windows between their release point and the house containing the guns, enter the courtyard from the East, and then enter the house from the courtyard. When in the house Hunter's squad would clear the interior, neutralize all threats, and seize the weapons. First and Second squads would surround the structure and ensure no one left and made sure no reinforcements could enter the house.

Hunter took a knee beside the truck, behind what he though was Henry. Sergeant Frost walked along each man in the line, his night vision goggles protruding from his face, confirming their identity. When he made it to Hunter he repeated the move.

"Hunter." He whispered.

Hunter nodded his head. Frost moved to the next Ranger in the line. As soon as he had made it through the string on men, ensuring that he had everyone, he moved quickly to the front to lead the squad to the house. They moved out.

The plan called for Alpha Team to breach the courtyard door and clear the small open area inside. Bravo Team would then breach the house door and clear the house, moving from room to room. Corry carried a sledge hammer from Alpha, while Lancaster carried one from Bravo. In the event the doors could not be opened with the sledge, Hunter carried two sticks of C-4 in his right leg cargo pocket. The fuse igniters, blasting caps, and ten seconds of time fuse were in one of the pouches on his LBE.

The movement went quick, stopping briefly at a small intersection and an alley. Next to the cache house they stopped. Hunter could hear a very light whisper coming from Sergeant Frost. *He must be letting the Platoon Leader and Platoon Sergeant know we are here,* he thought. Hunter scanned the target building then the buildings across the street. All was dark. They were stacked against the outside wall of the house. Hunter was second in line for Bravo team. The order went Henry, Hunter, Corry, and Brady. When they entered the house Corry would break the door in then Henry and Hunter would enter first. They would clear any rooms to the left of the team's movement. Corry and Brady would clear any rooms to the right. When entering a room Hunter would always go low and left, meaning he would cover anything in the lower part of the room while moving left and Henry would cover high and right, anything on the high side while moving right.

All the sudden a dog began to bark inside the target house. It was more of an alarmist yip. Apparently the dog had heard something outside the house and was now making sure everyone in the house knew it.

"GO!, GO!, GO!" Sergeant Frost yelled from his position at the front of the formation.

The clockwork execution that Hunter had trained for kicked in.

Corry immediately moved into the doorway and smashed open the thin metal gate. Alpha team quickly funneled through the opening. Bravo team moved up to the doorway.

"Crack, Crack, Crack" shots rang out in the night. "It was an M16" Hunter thought, "good - we still got the jump on them."

"GO!, GO!, GO!" Sergeant Frost yelled again, signaling them to enter the doorway and make their way to the back door.

The courtyard was small, maybe twenty feet by twenty feet. It was mostly barren, saved for what appeared to be junk piled up in one of the back corners and a large dark spot on the dirt. "The dog" Hunter thought, that's what the shots were.

Bravo team quickly flew to the back door of the house. Corry flew into the door with a massive Karate front snap kick. The thin door flew open with such force that Corry fell straight onto his back from the lack of resistance that should have repelled him rearward to land on his feet.

Henry jumped over top of Corry and entered the room first, Hunter followed close behind.

"Low and Left, Low and Left, Low and Left," Hunter repeated in his head as he entered the pitch black house.

There were several loud thumps and scurrying noises that echoed down from the second floor.

"Lights on," Henry said in a half whisper, half normal toned statement.

Hunter reached down with his non-firing hand and pressed the button on the end of the flashlight attached to his forearm assembly. A bright circle appeared in front of his weapon. It illuminated a short hallway that lead to the other end of the structure. *No bad guys, so far so good.* There was a doorway five feet in front of him to the left. Henry was already moving toward it.

Henry stopped for a split second outside the door to make sure Hunter was on his six. In the darkness outside the flashlight beams, Henry gave an almost imperceptible nod, and the two men entered the room.

The flash from the man's AK-74 was instant, lighting up the entire room in a strobe effect. The sound was deafening. The small room seemed to amplify the sound from all directions as the sound waves bounced off the walls. The man hadn't reacted quick enough to get a bead on Henry, he instead targeted the second shadow through the door. Hunter.

Hunter felt the heat and motion of bullets movement wiz past his head, splintering a section of the door jam just past his right cheek. His weapon, which was focused at the center of the room needed only to be adjusted slightly toward the flash. Instantaneously the light from the forearm assembly of his SAW illuminated a camouflage covered figure in the middle of the room as his index finger squeezed the trigger of his weapon hard.

Buzzzzzzit, ten rounds from the SAW impacted the figure in the chest, the force from the impact driving the man back against the wall hard. His weapon slumped as his body slid to the floor.

Hunter quickly scanned the rest of the left side of the room, there were no other soldiers.

"CLEAR!" Henry shouted from Hunter's right.

"CLEAR!" Hunter replied. "I've got one target down."

Sounds once again echoed from above. They're upstairs getting ready.

Shouts came from across the hall where Corry and Brady were clearing rooms. "CLEAR, I've got crates of weapons in here!"

Sergeant Frost's voice thundered down the hall, "Clear the rest of the house!"

Henry and Hunter exited the room and resumed moving down the hallway. Another door on the left, to the right of the open door was an open stairwell. A very dangerous situation for anyone clearing a house, the bad guys could shoot you from behind while you were in the room from either the stairs or the area on the opposite side of the stairs. Corry and Brady slid into the hallway just to the rear of Henry and Hunter.

Henry entered the second room with Hunter on his hip. Saved for some very old furniture the room was empty. More sounds settled down from the ceiling.

"CLEAR!"

"CLEAR!"

Across the hall Corry and Brady rounded the corner where the steps were and cleared the room on the other side.

"CLEAR!"

"CLEAR!"

"Bottom floor secured," Corry said from across the hall. More movement upstairs.

"I've got a lot of movement upstairs!" Hunter shouted pointing his weapon up the staircase as he entered the hallway from the cleared room. He could see an open doorway just to the left top of the stairs; a green shadow crossed the beam of light quickly. A hail of bullets rained down the stairs, pushing Henry and Hunter back into the room they had just cleared.

Holy shit, Hunter thought, *how are we going to get those bastards up the stairs?*

"I've got several personnel up the stairs," Henry responded as he squeezed the trigger of his M-16 aimed up the stairs

There was a slight pause and another hail of 7.62 rounds came tearing down the steps, shredding the wall next to the door opening that Henry and Hunter were in. Henry returned fire. Snap, Snap, Snap.

"I can't get a shot!" Henry yelled, "They have us pinned in this room!"

Hunter was against the wall directly behind Henry. He glanced over Henry's shoulder just as another volley of rounds came thundering down the stairwell. *How in the fuck are we going to get these bastards out of there?* It was one of classic things that were taught in urban warfare; go in from the top so you can flush them out of the downstairs door. The high ground has the advantage. This was one of those situations where they really didn't have the time to go in through the top, and thus the worse that could happen did. The enemy had a superior covered firing position that was elevated.

"I can't get a shot either!" Brady yelled from across the stairwell.

CRACK, CRACK, CRACK, CRACK, CRACK. The rounds rained down the steps.

From further down the hall Sergeant Frost called out, "Frag em!"

It was a great thought, Hunter contemplated. Throw a grenade up the stairs into the open doorway. The problem was; the frag had to make it directly into the doorway. If it didn't it would bounce off the walls and down the stairs toward the Rangers at the bottom of the steps. Very dangerous. The good part of the situation was that both teams had some cover in the rooms they were in.

"Hunter, you throw the frag. I'll cover you." Henry said as he looked over his left shoulder.

"Roger that Sergeant" Hunter replied.

Hunter quickly put his SAW on Safe, slung his weapon, and reached down on his LBE and unsnapped the button that held one of his grenades in place on the side of his 5.56 magazine pouch. He removed the round steel ball and held it in his right hand.

As he did this, Henry put several rounds up the stairs.

"Ready!" Hunter shouted above the sound of the M-16.

Henry stopped firing and changed magazines in his weapon. "Corry, Brady! We're gonna frag em, take cover!"

Another volley of rounds came down the steps.

"Make it good," Henry said in a monotone voice. "I'll cover you."

Hunter pulled the pin on the grenade.

It was going to be a very tricky shot. First he had to move to the bottom of the steps, completely exposing himself, then he would have to throw the frag on a straight line directly up the stairs so that it went into the open doorway at the top.

Everything seemed to go into slow motion; Henry scooted around the corner, firing directly up the stairs. Hunter stepped to his left and positioned himself at the base of the stair case. Hunter could see the red tracer round zinging up the stairs into the open doorway. He drew back his right arm and threw the grenade with all his might. The frag soared up the open stairwell hitting the door jam on the far side of the door and bounced in through the doorway.

"Frag out!" Hunter screamed as he moved back through the doorway he came through.

There was commotion on the second floor as people moved. "They must have seen or heard the frag," Hunter thought.

One...two...three, Hunter counted in his head as he un-slung his weapon.

BOOOOOOM! A thunderous roar shook the building.

Immediately Henry and Hunter were up the stairs.

The room was filled with a thick white smoke. As Hunter followed Henry through the doorway he went left and pushed his back against the wall. Through the beam of light protruding from the end of his SAW he could make out three bodies on the back wall in the center of the room. All three had their backs toward them, there were huge red gashes peppered across each where the shrapnel entered their bodies. Two were writhing in pain, shrieks radiating from their mouths. The third lay motionless.

Corry and Brady were up the stairs an instant later.

"I've got three down, room clear!" Henry shouted down the steps.

Hunter walked over and grabbed three AK-74s from each man's side, keeping his SAW trained on each as he did so. When he had the AK-74s collected he moved to the opposite end of the room and leaned them in the corner, pulling the magazine from each and ejecting the round in the chamber. Two of the enemy personnel continued to scream as Corry and Brady rolled each over and checked for any additional weapons.

Sergeant Frost entered the room. As he walked in he was keying the mic on his radio. "Red one, this is red three. . . objective clear, I say again objective clear. We have two enemy K.I.A., and two enemy W.I.A. We are gonna need a medic up here for the two enemy W.I.A."

The rest of the platoon searched the grounds and found several boxes of new H & K MP5s in an above ground fuel oil tank to go with the several crates on AK-74s inside the structure.

CHAPTER 31

Emil was furious. It seemed that his entire regiment had either been killed or was hiding somewhere in the hills and his Presedente was nowhere to be found. There was one thread of hope that he had to hold on to, his entire platoon was briefed on a contingency plan the week prior in case the Americans had attacked. In the plan, if the units were scattered by American forces they were to link up exactly one week from the date of the attack at a house in Altos del Diablo, a suburb of Panama City. They would then receive orders on how to conduct gorilla attacks on the invaders and get additional weapons.

Emil made his way out of the hills and onto Carreterra Interamericana Route one, leading to Panama City. The highway was deserted, so he began walking toward the city. He didn't mind, a little walk in the dark would help him clear his head and plan his moves once he made his way into the big city. It also made it easy to detect any cars coming down the highway. When a car would come along, he would just flag it down and take it.

After a half hour, Emil could hear the distant sound of a car's engine heading his way. He took his AK-74 off his shoulder and stretched his neck from side to side. "This should be easy" he thought. "If they are Americans I will kill everyone in the car, if they are Panamanian I will take the car and make them walk." He positioned himself in the center of the road and pointed his weapon down the highway toward the sound. He was positioned on the thoroughfare about 50 meters from where there was a bend in the road. The car would not be able to see him until they rounded the corner, thus not giving them time to stop far away and turn around. If they didn't stop he would just put a few bullets through the front window and make them stop. He wouldn't mind killing a few people in the car; he just didn't want to sit in the glass and blood that the engagement would generate.

Seconds later the car sped around the corner, lights flashing directly on Emil in the center of the road. The vehicle immediately slammed on the breaks and skidded to a stop five meters in front of Emil. A male voice screamed from inside the car in Spanish, "What the hell are you doing?"

Emil casually walked up to the driver's window and stuck the gun barrel inside. "Get out!"

"Hell no you fucking idiot, I am a very important man. Get the hell out of my way." The Mercedes lurched forward as the man began to hit the gas.

It only took a fraction of a second to pull the trigger on the AK-74. A single bullet ripped through the man's temple, disintegrating the entire right side of his head. Blood and brain matter flew across the passenger seat of the luxury sedan. The car rolled for twenty meters before coming to a stop on the right side of the road in the dense underbrush.

Emil walked to the car and opened the door. The man's body was hunched over the passenger seat, a massive amount of blood was still pouring from the wound on the man's head, pooling in the seat. Emil grabbed the body by the shoulders and pulled it out onto the road. He searched the man's pockets and removed his wallet taking out a stack of bills from inside. After depositing the bills in his own pocket, he lifted the body off the road and through it into the ditch on the opposite side. Once he returned to the car he got in, adjusted the seat forward, and drove off toward the city.

With the Mercedes he would be able to go as far as the Bridge of the Americas, there he knew there would be a check point for sure. Emil would have to ditch the car somewhere on this side of the Canal, head north and find a way across by boat.

35 minutes later Carreterra Interamericana Route one turned into Via Panamericana, after just a few minutes on Via Panamericana Emil could see the Bridge of the Americas in the distance. He took a left on a road called Wahoo into a small town called Rodman. He parked the car at the end of the first of three piers that jetted out into the canal. He could see several small boats tied along the south side of the pier, the other two piers contained large sea going vessels.

Emil made his way to the pier and quickly found a row boat tied along side of a larger fishing vessel. He quietly slipped over the fishing vessel and made his way onto the row boat. Minutes later he was crossing the water headed toward Altos del Diablo, the place where he would meet his compadres and exact his plot for revenge.

The water was generally calm and it was easy to row to the other side. Emil made it across the waterway in a little over 20 minutes, avoiding a massive pier that was positioned directly on the other side of the canal, landing on the bank slightly downstream from the opposite side where he started. He scurried out of the boat and up to land, letting the boat float away in the night. He moved through the undergrowth that was on the bank and found himself on Reseau street, a street he recognized. Moving quickly he headed north on Reseau to Yarns, then east on Yarns to Diablo. One block north on Diablo and he found the house he was looking for.

He went to the door and knocked softly three times. "Si" a voice from the other side responded.

"Emil Rojo Rodriguez"

The door opened to let him in.

Inside he found twelve soldiers he knew, a cache of weapons and ammunition, and his mission. He would defend La Joyita prison just north of Altos del Diablo.

CHAPTER 32

"This one should be interesting," Sergeant Frost smiled as he back briefed his squad. They knelt in a tight circle at the edge of taxiway next to the silent Black Hawks that would soon take then into their next engagement.

"Corry, what's the fast rope exit order?"

Corry visibly straightened, his eyes glaring in the moon light. "My door is, Hunter, Sergeant Henry, Me, Chambers, and the 60 crew."

"Good," Sergeant Frost turned toward Hunter, "When do you kick the rope out?"

"When the crew chief tells me Sergeant," Hunter shot back quickly.

"No Shit," Sergeant Frost said with a slight chuckle, "When will he tell you?"

"After the mini-gunners on the Black Hawk's sides take out the guard towers on all four corners of the compound and we are hovering just outside the South East corner of the building."

"What is the contingency if the drop zone for roping in is obscured or blocked?"

"Air land in a clearing two blocks South of the prison in an open lot, then haul ass to the prisons south gate," Hunter finished his statement with a nod, knowing that he was right.

This was the way they always did it, any down time before the mission they would go over it again and again until everyone knew exactly what to do in all situations. They would physically practice it over and over and then they would back brief like this for what seemed like hours. It worked though; Hunter couldn't remember a mission where he didn't know what to do in any contingency.

The sun had set several hours ago, and the night was starting to cool a bit. It seemed simple enough; Rope in, Clear, Crush the resistance.

Hunter was tired, completely tired. Not as much physically, but his soul, his spirit, his being. *Maybe it's finally time. I just want to go with honor.*

Is my destiny fulfilled? The whine of the Black Hawk engines cut into the dusk. Within minutes the rotors were turning. The squad stood and waited to board the helicopter.

The crew chief appeared in the open side door of the aircraft and signaled the squad to load. Hunter was first. They had rehearsed loading order and position in the bird until he knew it by heart the prior night, so he instinctively moved to the front left side of the cargo area in the rear of the Black Hawk. The helicopter's seats had been folded up so that there was nothing in the cargo area. Hunter took the end of his sling rope that had been attached around his body and clipped the snap link into one of the cargo rings in the floor. Ten seconds later the entire squad was inside the Black Hawk. The helicopter majestically lifted off the ground, and shot skyward as it moved off in the north east sky.

The flight time was very short, seven minutes to be exact. So one minute into the flight the Crew Chief gave the signal for six minutes. As Hunter looked out the open door he could see the lights of Panama City reflecting off the waters of the canal. The lights blurred in the water as the aircraft flew through the sky at over 150 miles per hour. The flight pattern took them to the north west side of the city and then would loop around the Miraflores Lock and approach the prison from the north. Hunter could feel the sharp bank and then the sensation of falling out of the sky as the Black Hawk dropped to nap of the earth flying for the assault.

The crew chief, who was positioned between the two gunners turned and gave the signal for 30 seconds. A muffled shout came in unison from the front four Rangers in the aircraft "THIRTY SECONDS!"

Hunter reached down between his knees and unhooked the snap link. Seconds after unsnapping the dangling safety rope there was a huge flash and a thunderous roar as both of the side gunners started firing. The bright flash took Hunter by surprise. The aircraft was banking hard to the rear to make a quick stop.

The crew chief, who was staring back into the main cabin, nodded as he received the orders from the pilots through his radio speakers in his helmet. The man pointed at Hunter and Donaldson to kick the ropes out.

Hunter kicked the coiled rope out the door as hard as he could. It quickly snaked out to the ground. He watched the rope that had a chem.-light on the end, touch the courtyard below. He immediately leaped out the door and began sliding down the rope like a fireman's pole slowing himself only slightly with his gloved hands.

At that millisecond the rotors from the helicopter began to slice into some tree branches that were overhanging the prison walls. The strikes began to pull the aircraft into the trees. The pilot did the only thing he could do to save his helicopter from crashing into the trees; he pulled up hard on the stick and gave the collective full power. The bird leaped up and the crew chief grabbed at both Donaldson and Hunter to stop them from going onto the rope, he reached Donaldson in time to grab his arm a split second before he leapt out the door, his right hand grasp at air as Hunter was already on his way down the rope.

When Hunter reached the end of the rope he was startled to find that the rope was not on the ground anymore, he freefell into the darkness of the courtyard landing in a PLF (Parachute Landing Fall) on the dirt of the courtyard ten feet below the now dangling rope.

The Pilot, fearing that the ropes would become entangled in the tree limbs, cut the ropes away. The ropes fell from the mounts above the open doors of the Black Hawk, landing in the courtyard with Hunter, leaving Hunter in the La Joyita prison alone.

CHAPTER 33

Emil heard a massive sound coming from the opposite end of the recently abandoned Prison. It sounded like an explosive saw was cutting the building open.

"They are here," he commented to the two other men in the room inside the administrative building on the southern section of the prison.

In this section of the La Joyita prison Emil, who ended up as the ranking Non-Commissioned Officer, had deployed the twelve men that had made it to the safe house around the prison in two man teams. He placed teams in the four guard towers that were posted at the each corner of the prison, hoping to catch the enemy in a deadly cross fire as they approached the prison from any direction.

His strategy was simple; deploy his men in such a way that he would kill as many of the American Pigs as possible. He thought the best way to do this would be to put them in the guard towers so they could see both inside and outside the prison walls. As he ran down the hall that connected the main prison to the courtyard a sinking feeling began to grow in his stomach. "What if they destroyed the guard towers with their helicopters?" he thought. He took an immediate right when he reached the door to the courtyard and ran another 25 meters to the stairwell that lead to the south west guard tower. He scaled the steps two at a time until he reached the second floor where a ladder led the rest of the way to the observation point through a trap door in the ceiling.

"What is happening up there?" he shouted to his men above.

"A helicopter just rained bullets on the two far guard towers, they are destroyed!" a voice from above responded.

Emil climbed the latter as fast as he could, pounding on the trap door. The door flew open as Estes, the soldier immediately above, pulled up the cover to the opening. Emil hurried through the opening. As he entered Rondo, the second soldier in the tower, began shooting at the now retreating helicopter.

Emil reviewed the scene as he popped his head above the waist high wall of the tower. He could see that both of the north towers were decimated, his men surly dead. The helicopter was now flying away in the distance, a shadowy wraith in the night.

"At least I still have my two south towers," he thought.

CHAPTER 34

The sound from the mini-guns had stopped abruptly about half way down the rope. Now as Hunter rolled into a prone firing position, taking the slung SAW from his shoulder as he tumbled.

"Target, target, target," he thought as he scanned to the south side of the prison. He searched low then high, that's when he saw the first gunner from the south eastern most tower spraying rounds at the Black Hawk, the green tracers streaming toward the now retreating aircraft.

Buzzzzzzzzzzzzzzit. Hunter unloaded a burst at the figure, aiming at his feet originally knowing that the rising barrel of his SAW would hit the figure center mass. The shadowy figure dropped over the safety rail and smashed into the courtyard below.

As the body fell Hunter suddenly felt very alone. He looked to his right rear just in time to see the rope fall to the ground in an unorganized heap.

"What the hell," he thought. He quickly looked over his left shoulder to find the other doors rope in the same condition.

CRACK, CRACK, CRACK. Three bullets ripped at the ground just in front of Hunter's position. He rolled over his left shoulder and leapt to his feet in a full sprint toward a small building along the outer wall of the facility. Hunter dove behind the building just as several more rounds impacted just behind him.

Suddenly there were rounds coming from two directions, emanating from the south end of the prison. Sustained burst were impacting the building Hunter was behind.

"Thank God this building was here or I would be dead for sure," Hunter thought. He looked up to his rear to see the Black Hawk gliding away in the night, between the two guard towers that were smoking heaps of debris. After thirty seconds of bullets rapidly hitting the building he was behind, the firing stopped. He glanced around the edge of the building,

only exposing the side of his face for a fraction of a second. In that time he could see that there was another person in the south eastern guard tower, he didn't want to stick his head out far enough to see if the second source of fire was coming from the south west guard tower, he was pretty sure it was.

Hunter took a deep breath and stood, knowing that he was about to expose himself, pointed his SAW skyward in preparation for firing around the corner, and made his move. He rapidly swung his machine gun around the corner, firing as he came around. He directed his fire at the guard tower.

Buzzzzzzzzzzzzzzzzzzzzzzzzzzzzzzzzzzzzit. After a sustained burst Hunter could see the green tracers coming directly at his location as his red tracers formed a steady line of bullets toward the enemy's position. He quickly pulled back around the corner to the safety of the small block building, the rounds ricocheting off the corner of the building. He waited for the barrage to stop, he then whipped around the corner and administered another wave of rounds.

Buzzzzzzzzzzzzzzzzzzzzzzzzzzzzzzzzzzzit. He lead his red tracer rounds to where the figure he had seen laying on his stomach in his last look was, pummeling the area. Hunter moved back around the corner and waited. One second, two seconds, three seconds. Nothing happened. He repeated the motion and unloaded another wave in the same direction.

Buzzzzzzzzzzzzzzit. Hunter's SAW stopped firing as he ran out of rounds in his first 200 round drum. He pulled back around the corner and dropped to his knee, rapidly pulling one of his two remaining drums from his LBE. He flipped open the feed tray cover, ejected the empty drum, and rapidly snapped on the fresh container of belt ammo in one fluid motion. He then pulled the first few rounds from the drum and inserted them into the feed tray and snapped the cover shut, pulling the charging handle to the rear and releasing it to seat the first round on the belt.

"*What the hell happened to the rest of my squad?*" he wondered. He waited a few more seconds, no sound came. He glanced back around the corner, no rounds came. Nothing was moving in the guard tower. "*I must have got the little bastard.*" Taking a few extra seconds he surveyed the scene. He could see a door on the ground floor half way between the two towers. The tower he had been firing at was quiet, but he couldn't see far enough around the building to see what the other tower was doing.

Hunter quickly formulated a plan. They would soon come for him, especially since he was pinned down in an area where they could send a whole platoon after him through the door on the courtyard level, but he wasn't going to let it happen. *This will be the day that I die, this will be the day that I die...* He grabbed his one HC smoke grenade from his left shoulder harness on his LBE and pulled the pin. He stepped back away from the wall of the building and lofted the HC smoke grenade over the top of the building toward the south west guard tower. There was a small "pop" as the smoke grenade ignited. He looked down at his only four fragmentation grenades and pulled one from his container on the side of one of his 30 round magazine pouches attached to his LBE. The 30 round magazine pouches were full of chem-lights and flex cuffs, things he thought he would need on this mission, he now wished he had filled them with 30 round mags of 5.56 ammo since he had already went through a full drum. *"But who knew I would end up in the prison alone."*

Hunter pulled the pin, stepped back away from the wall and threw the heavy round fragmentation grenade as hard as he could over the building in the direction of the guard tower. As soon as he released the grenade he moved back up against the building and glanced around the corner to make sure no one had come out the door. "One thousand one, one thousand two, one thousand three, one thousand four," Hunter brought his weapon back up to his shoulder and dug his feet in as if at the starting line of a race. "One thousand five," there was a monstrous explosion as the grenade went off.

Hunter took off as fast as he could in a sprint toward the door. As he cleared the side of the building he could see a huge cloud of white smoke obscuring the guard tower. He squeezed the trigger of his SAW tight and aimed at where the guard tower should be.

Buzzzzzzzzzzzzzzzzzzzzzzzzzzzzzzzzzzzzzzzzzzzzzzzzzzzzzzzzzzit. He held the trigger for over half the distance to the door, covering the 20 meters quickly. Hunter then turned his weapon toward the door and pulled the trigger again.

Buzzzzzzzzzzzzzzzzzzzzzzzzzzzzzzzzzzzzzzzzzzzzzzzzzzzzzzzzzzit. The door splintered as the bullets tore through its inch thick wood. Most of the fire was focused near the door handle. As Hunter reached the door he put his left shoulder down and pulled his machine gun to his rear as he smashed through the entrance into a long hallway that appeared to go the length of the south side of the prison. He rolled once and burst back onto his feet, weapon poised to engage targets.

The long hall was empty. Hunter looked to his left to see a stairwell that was empty, and then he looked right to see an identical stairwell, empty as well. "Which way would they come from?" He knew he was in an extremely bad position. So he did what he was trained to do, when in doubt, assault. He chose the long hallway in front of him.

CHAPTER 35

The bullets from the courtyard radiated up from the flat floor below, Emil could see them hitting his south east tower. The red tracers seemed to make a straight line toward his compadres. He raised his AK-74 and began firing at the shadow on the ground.

As he unleashed his first three bullets, he could see the shape move behind a block building on the side of the courtyard like a ghost in the night. Emil unloaded the rest of his magazine at the corner of the building. Rondo and Estes did the same.

"Keep up the fire," Emil demanded as he turned to lift the door in the middle of the floor. When he had the door opened he slid down the ladder, closing the trap door cover behind him.

"The pigs were in the compound," he would have to crush them before they got out of the courtyard on the first floor.

The second the door shut a stream of red tracer bullets poured into the opposite tower, stopping the fire that the other soldiers were pouring into the courtyard. After a slight lull, there was a soft pop and a billow of white smoke began wafting upward in front of the guard tower, obscuring Estes and Rondo's line of sight to the floor of the courtyard.

"Can you see?" Rondo asked.

"No!" Estes answered. As he finished the word, there was a large clank as something heavy flew into the confines of the tower.

Rondo and Estes could only look at each other as the realization of what the object was.

The explosion from the fragmentation grenade ripped both of them apart in a cascade of metal shards, throwing both bodies over the waist high wall. Estes broken body landing in the courtyard, Rondo's outside the compound between the outer and the inner fences of the prison.

Emil heard the large explosion above him as he began down the steps. He turned and retraced his route, quickly scaling the ladder again. When he forced the trap door open he was greeted by acrid smoke and an area littered with block shards and blood. Rondo and Estes were nowhere to be found. Bullets immediately began to shower the area. Emil dropped back down the ladder to safety. He could hear machine gun fire coming from down the stairwell.

They were inside the prison itself.

CHAPTER 36

Hunter sprinted down the hall toward another door 25 meters away. This door looked much weaker than the outside door so he made a split decision, go through at full speed. He put down his shoulder as he had done earlier and hit it at full speed. The door flew completely off it's hinges as the force from the onrush was too great.

Hunter stumbled and fell to his knees, bringing his weapon back to his front. He squeezed the trigger as he brought the SAW around; rounds covered the room from right to left.

Buzzzzzzzzzzzzzzzzzzzzzzzzit.

In the room the two PDF soldiers were startled by the intrusion. Both were facing the door as it broke open, but only had their AK's at waist level. The immediate fire from Hunter's SAW hit both men in the chest, throwing them rearward, and splattering blood against the wall behind them.

The first soldier fell two meters in front of Hunter, the second just to his left behind a desk that was positioned in the center of the room.

Hunter swung his weapon back to the first individual and squeezed the trigger.

Buzzzzzit.

A short burst hit the body, again tearing a hole in the man's sternum. Hunter rose to his feet and pulled the trigger again aiming his weapon over the desk. After the first few rounds he scurried around the desk as he fired.

Buzzzzzzzzzzzzzzzzzzzzzzzzzzzzzit.

The second deadly burst found the other soldiers body, disintegrating the man's head.

Hunter was standing in some kind of office, papers were styrene across the desk, while the rest of the room appeared to be in disarray, now especially that the door was ripped down lying on the floor.

From the corner of his eye Hunter saw movement down the hall that he had just came from. He turned his weapon to face the target and pulled the trigger, putting some rounds down the length of the hall.

Buzzzit. The SAW stopped firing, out of ammo. Hunter dove behind the desk and pushed up on the front edge, flipping it on its side to give him some semblance of cover.

AK-74 bullets came crashing against the desktop, ripping pieces of wood out as they came, flakes from the desk showering Hunter. He grabbed his final drum of 5.56 ammunition and loaded his weapon from the sitting position, the 7.62 AK rounds tearing through the desk just four inches above his head. "*Fuck, fuck, fuck,*" he thought as he snapped the feed tray cover shut and pulled hard on the charging handle. He turned to face the desk as the enemy bullets paused, grabbed a fragmentation grenade from his LBE and pulled hard on the pin. The pin pulled out and Hunter released the spoon on the frag.

Everything seemed to go into slow motion.

The grenade spoon majestically flew off and arched toward the floor.

Two more AK bullets flew through the desk, this time missing Hunter's head by half an inch.

"One thousand one, one thousand two," Hunter began to count, "ONE THOUSAND THREE!" He moved his head with his Kevlar helmet up just high enough to see the top of the door frame, drew his arm to the rear and tossed the frag over the desk, through the door way, and down the hall. As he released the orb, his head snapped to the rear as a 7.62 round struck the very top of his helmet. The inertia from the bullet knocked him completely backwards, so that he landed on his back, flat on the floor, inches away from the soldier he had just neutralized. Everything went black for a second.

The grenade made it through the doorway and bounced against the left wall, then back to the right, making it 20 meters down the hall.

Emil, who was firing at the desk, saw the object coming down the corridor just as the last bullet of his magazine fired from the barrel of his AK 74. He leapt to his left toward the safety of the hallway leading to the guard tower steps just as a deafening explosion rocked the entire structure.

Emil fell to the ground around the corner from the grenade, shrapnel missing his feet by inches. The pressure from the explosion burst his ear drum on his mangled ear as he hit the floor. A constant ringing sound filled his head as blood soaked his dirty bandage that was already covering the ear.

Hunter regained consciousness a moment later; he scurried back to his knees and unbuckled his now grooved helmet, pulling it off and dropping it on the ground. He pointed his SAW down the hall as he lifted up. As his head rose above the table he sighted down the corridor into the smoke and floating debris left by the grenade and pulled the trigger. Nothing happened. Without thinking he began to pull the charging handle to the rear to remove the blockage, but the handle would not move. He looked down at his weapon to see the entire feed assembly was dented in from a bullet impact. *"Did I get them, did I get them?"* His mind raced furiously. *"What if I didn't get them? I'm a sitting duck, my SAW is done!"*

Reaching for another grenade, he pulled the pin and waited for the smoke to clear from the hallway.

Emil stumbled to his feet and shook his head from side to side, trying to stop the ringing. Blinking his eyes, he released the 7.62 magazine from the AK and popped in a new one. He pulled the charging handle to the rear and shook his head again as he released it. *"These bastards are going to pay!"* He screamed and rounded the corner to assault down the now littered hallway.

Hunter heard the scream and immediately threw the fragmentation grenade through the doorway and down the hall. He withdrew his combat knife from its holder.

Rounding the corner Emil pulled the trigger of his AK-74. Three bullets flew down the corridor through the now clearing smoke into the office. He took one step when he saw the grenade coming down the hallway, bouncing on the tiled floor. The heavy metal object hit his left foot and ricocheted to hit the wall of the hallway. Shifting his motion, he turned and ran toward the safety of the hallway in which he just came.

The first two bullets missed Hunter by inches over his left shoulder, the third grazed his right shoulder, cutting a strip from his uniform and making a three inch gash in his deltoid. The momentum of the projectile spun him to the right. He landed on his stomach facing the opposite direction, still grasping the knife in his left hand. *This will be the day that I die, this will be the day that I die. Those good old boys were drinking whisky and rye, singing this will be the day that I die.*

Boooooooooooom. Another massive explosion rocked the building.

Hunter's adrenaline was pumping so hard he didn't feel the wound in his shoulder or notice the even louder ringing in his ears from being so close to the explosion of the grenades. He leap to his feet and began sprinting down the hall, a scowl covering his smeared camouflage covered face. *"These fuckers aren't going to take me alive."*

Traversing the corner, Emil had time to run half way down the corridor leading to the tower. When the grenade went off, he was well out of harms way. As the sound of the explosion echoed through the halls, he turned and ran back the way he came. "*I will kill these American pigs!*" Nearing the corner again, he drew his AK up tight in his shoulder and prepared to fire when he made the turn.

Hunter was going to make the turn around the corner at full speed. "*If they're there, I'll go for the heads to take out as many as I can.*" He pumped his arms back and forth as sped down the hallway.

As both men reached the corner they collided with an audible "smack". The momentum from Hunter's 25 meter sprint carried Emil through the door on the rear wall and outside into the prison yard, both soldiers loosing their weapons. The AK-74 and the combat knife clamored onto the tile floor inside the hall.

Both stood up slowly five meters apart, each trying to catch his breath.

Hunter, who was wearing a flak vest, unbuckled his LBE, then reached up and undid the Velcro that held the vest together in the front. "*I'm not going to keep this heavy vest on and go hand to hand with this guy,*" all the while watching his adversary.

Emil stared directly into Hunters eyes, rapidly sucking in as much oxygen as he could.

Hunter cautiously pulled the vest and LBE off one shoulder, then the other, slowly dropping the heavy piece of equipment to his right.

"Come on mother fucker." Hunter slowly put his right hand out in front of his body and motioned toward his chest with his fingers. "Let's see how bad you really are."

Emil swung hard with his right fist in a large roundhouse punch.

Hunter quickly stepped toward Emil's body, raised his arm high, and caught the motion with his left upper arm, pulling his elbow down hard, locking Emil's arm under his own. With his right hand he went for the throat. As his fingers reached his wind pipe, he clamped down on it with massive force.

Emil grasped for the hand around his throat with his left hand and pulled with all his might, struggling to release the iron grip. He tried to throw his head forward, but the hand around his neck wouldn't allow the motion. He stomped his left foot down, hoping to impact Hunter's toes, but the close proximity and body positions didn't allow the impact. Emil frantically went for Hunter's eyes, but Hunter raised his right elbow, effectively shielding his eyes.

Emil's eyes rolled back in his head and everything faded to black.

Hunter held his grip for another minute to make sure he was dead, and then dropped the lifeless body to the ground.

A second later Brady burst through the open door followed by the entire squad. They spread out on both sides of the opening. They had breached both sets of wire on the outside of the prison and had entered through the doors at the front. "CLEAR!"

Sergeant Frost shuffled up to Hunter. "You OK?"

Hunter looked into his eyes, paused a moment then nodded, "Hooah Sergeant."

BOOK 2

BOOK 2

CHAPTER 1

A Chance For Reconcilliation, The Desert

"All I wanted was a mission, and for my sins they gave me one."

Jamie L. Chester served on active duty in the United States Military from 1988 to 1992, then in the National Guard from 1992 to 1998. In that time he participated in Operation Just Cause in Panama, Operation Desert Shield / Desert Storm in Iraq, and was part of the 1996 Olympic Security Team in Atlanta. He now resides in Ohio and enjoys spending time with his wife and three children.

Jamie would love to hear from his readers at rangerjambo@yahoo. com.